Forget Me Knot

Garden Girls Cozy Mystery Series Book 13

Hope Callaghan

hopecallaghan.com

Copyright © 2016

All rights reserved.

This book is a work of fiction. Although places mentioned may be real, the characters, names and incidents, and all other details are products of the author's imagination and are fictitious. Any resemblance to actual events or actual persons, living or dead is purely coincidental.

No part of this publication may be copied, reproduced in any format, by any means, electronic or otherwise, without prior consent from the copyright owner and publisher of this book. The only exception is brief quotations in printed reviews.

Visit my website for new releases and special offers: **hopecallaghan.com**

Thank you, Peggy Hyndman, Cindi Graham and Wanda Downs for taking the time to preview *Forget Me Knot,* for the extra sets of eyes and for catching all my mistakes.

Free Cozy Mysteries Newsletter

Sign up for my Free Cozy Mysteries Newsletter to get free and discounted books, giveaways & soon-to-be-released books!

hopecallaghan.com/newsletter

TABLE OF CONTENTS

Free Cozy Mysteries Newsletter ii

Meet The Author v

Foreword vi

Chapter 1 1

Chapter 2 12

Chapter 3 27

Chapter 4 44

Chapter 5 58

Chapter 6 68

Chapter 7 81

Chapter 8 92

Chapter 9 103

Chapter 10 111

Chapter 11 117

Chapter 12 129

Chapter 13 142

Chapter 14 .... *154*

Chapter 15 .... *167*

Chapter 16 .... *176*

Chapter 17 .... *189*

Chapter 18 .... *198*

Chapter 19 .... *206*

Chapter 20 .... *220*

Chapter 21 .... *230*

Chapter 22 .... *240*

Chapter 23 .... *251*

Chapter 24 .... *263*

Chapter 25 .... *277*

Chapter 26 .... *286*

Chapter 27 .... *294*

Chicken Tortilla Casserole Recipe *298*

Meet The Author

Hope Callaghan is an author who loves to write Christian books, especially Christian Mystery and Cozy Mystery books. She has written more than 40 mystery books (and counting) in four series.

Born and raised in a small town in West Michigan, she now lives in Florida with her husband.

She is the proud mother of one daughter and a stepdaughter and stepson. When she's not doing the thing she loves best - writing books - she enjoys cooking, traveling and reading books.

Hope loves to connect with her readers! Connect with her today!

Visit **hopecallaghan.com** for special offers, free books, and soon-to-be-released books!

Email: **hope@hopecallaghan.com**

Facebook:
https://www.facebook.com/hopecallaghanauthor/

Foreword

Dear Reader,

I would like to personally thank you for purchasing this book and also to let you know that a portion of all my book sales go to support missions which proclaim the Good News of Jesus Christ.

My prayer is that you will be blessed by reading my stories and knowing that you are helping to spread the Gospel of the Lord.

With more than thirty mystery books (and counting) in four series published, I hope you will have as much fun reading them as I have writing them!

May God Bless You!

Sincerely,

Author Hope Callaghan

"Many are the plans in a person's heart, but it is the LORD's purpose that prevails." Proverbs 19:21 NIV

Chapter 1

Gloria Rutherford-Kennedy rested her forehead against the steering wheel of her car and adjusted her cell phone so it was closer to her ear. "Annabelle is dead!"

"What do you mean she's dead?" Gloria's husband, Paul, asked.

"Well, I'm sitting in my car and just tried to start it. All it does is make a grinding noise like…err, err, err," she explained. "It's not the battery. That seems to be fine."

"Better call Gus to tow it to his shop." Gus Smith and his wife, Mary Beth, owned Smith Auto Repair, the auto repair shop in the small town of Belhaven where Gloria and her husband, Paul, lived.

Paul paused, certain his new bride wouldn't like what he was about to say next. "Perhaps it's time to put Annabelle to rest. She's been a great car but she's getting up there in miles and is going to start nickel and diming us to death."

Gloria refused to consider getting rid of her beloved Annabelle and quickly dismissed his suggestion. "I'll give Gus a call." Gloria said good-bye, disconnected the line and dialed Gus's number.

"Smith Auto Repair. Gus speaking."

"Hi Gus. It's Gloria. Annabelle is being finicky this morning and won't start." She briefly repeated what she had just told Paul.

Gus told her he would be there shortly. After telling him she'd be waiting, Gloria pressed the *end call* button to disconnect the line before climbing out of the car and heading to the back porch to wait for Gus and his tow truck to arrive.

Memorial Day, along with Andrea's engagement celebration, was right around the corner. Gloria didn't have time for car trouble. Paul and she had also planned a family get-together, a combination clean-out-the-barns and house party for their children and grandchildren to come over and sort through the stacks of stuff Paul and Gloria no longer needed since they'd recently married and combined households.

Many of the things Gloria had set aside were family heirlooms and items with sentimental value from not only her first husband, James's, side of the family, but hers, too.

There were also cherished toys and clothes she'd saved from when her children were young and she wanted to make sure the treasures were not accidentally mixed in with Paul's things that he planned to pass onto his own children.

Also in the works was a party the Garden Girls were planning, a combination Memorial Day cookout and engagement celebration for Brian and Andrea's recent engagement, which had been put on the backburner while the girls had taken a recent cruise.

Andrea had insisted they hold the festive party at her place, her mini-mansion they had dubbed Magnolia Mansion. It would be Andrea's chance to show off her beautiful home. She had plenty of room and, for once, Gloria was happy to pass the baton and let someone else host a get-together.

Gus and his wrecker turned into the drive. He pulled past the car, backed up so he was directly behind Annabelle, and then climbed out of the driver's seat.

Gloria hopped off the porch and met him near the back. "I hope it's not too serious," she fretted as she watched Gus place two hooks under the bumper of the car.

"Annabelle is getting up there," Gus commented. "What year is she?"

"1989," Gloria said. "It was a good year." She remembered the first time she'd first laid eyes on Annabelle, how James had surprised her when he brought the brand spanking new car home. It had been love at first sight.

A lump formed in Gloria's throat and she swallowed hard. She knew it was silly to get emotional over a car, but Annabelle was a part of her life and she had many fond memories.

Gus flipped a switch on the back of the wrecker, and Annabelle creaked and groaned as the hooks lifted her back end off the ground. "Got a loaner I can let you borrow for a few days. I bought a *be-yoot* down at the auto auction in Grand Rapids a few days ago. Nice ride. 2015 Ford SUV with low miles. The owner got into a little fender bender, and then the finance company took it back after he stopped making payments."

Gus leaned against the side of his wrecker and studied Annabelle thoughtfully. "I got it all fixed up, ready to sell. Why don't you drive it for a couple days while I look at Annabelle? You might be surprised at how much you'll like driving something newer."

Gloria doubted it. She loved Annabelle, but she wasn't about to look a gift horse in the mouth. "That would be perfect. Of course, I'll pay you a rental fee."

"Nah!" Gus waved his hand. "You're like family Gloria. I can't charge you for the loan. Hop in and I'll take you down to the shop where you can pick up the vehicle."

"Thanks, Gus. You're a doll. Let me grab my purse off the porch." After grabbing her purse, Gloria headed to the wrecker's passenger side door and started to climb in when she noticed a huge dark splotch on the seat. It looked like a grease stain.

Gus noticed her look, reached behind the driver's seat and pulled out a piece of cardboard. He set the cardboard on the seat. "Sorry about the seat. I don't think it'll get on your clothes, but just to be safe you can sit on this."

Gloria grinned as she stared at the cardboard. At least it looked clean. She settled onto the piece of cardboard and reached for her seatbelt.

The interior of the wrecker reeked of motor oil and gasoline. Gloria's eyes began to burn. She gulped a big breath of air and began gagging at the overpowering smell.

Gus flipped a switch to open the windows. "Sorry about the smell. Wes, the young kid I hired to help me out after school, accidentally tipped over a gas can and it spilled on the floor." He shook his head. "Kids."

Once the wrecker was on the road and they started driving, fresh air filled the cab and the smell vanished. They had rounded the curves near the edge of the lake leading into town when Gloria heard the sound of sirens. She glanced in the rearview mirror and spotted a police car bearing down on them.

Gus noticed, too, and quickly pulled onto the side of the road as the car whizzed by. "Uh-oh. That can't be good."

They had just pulled back onto the road when they heard another siren. It was an ambulance. Again, Gus pulled off and let the ambulance by. "I wonder what is going on."

When they reached the repair shop, Gus pulled in front of the service bay door and climbed out of the tow truck. Gloria trailed behind, noticing a newer, silver SUV parked in the lot. She correctly guessed it was the loaner vehicle.

Mary Beth, Gus's wife, was behind the counter. She looked up as they stepped inside. "Hi Gloria. I'd like to say it's nice to see you, but I'm sure you're not thrilled to see me."

Gloria placed her purse on the counter and sighed heavily. "I hate car problems." She glanced at Gus, who was fumbling with the keys on the rack behind the counter. "Gus is an angel for dropping everything to help me out. He's even going to loan me the new SUV you picked up."

"It's an awesome ride," Mary Beth said. "You're gonna fall in love with it once you drive it. If I didn't have my nearly-new sedan, I would keep it for myself."

Gus handed Gloria a set of keys. "If you want, I'll show you a few things before you take off."

Gloria waved good-bye to Mary Beth and then followed Gus to the SUV. He opened the door. "Hop in."

The first thing Gloria noticed was how roomy it seemed. The second thing she noticed was the smell...new and leather. Gus was right. The SUV was like new.

She took the keys from Gus and began searching for the ignition.

"Nope. Don't need those. This is one of those fancy push button vehicles." Gus showed her how to start the car and Gloria shook her head. "This is too luxurious for me, not that Annabelle isn't luxury, she's vintage luxury."

After showing Gloria a few more of the vehicle's bells and whistles, he sent her on her way. She began to back out of the parking spot and then tapped the horn.

Gus, who was halfway to the door, made his way back over.

"What if I get into an accident and total this thing?" she asked.

Gus shoved his hands in his pockets and grinned. "You break it, you buy it," he joked, and then waved a hand dismissively. "Nah! It's already insured."

She nodded. "Now that you mention it, I think my auto insurance would cover damages, too." Gloria waved to Gus and headed toward town, anxious to find out where the police car and ambulance had gone.

Chapter 2

It took Gloria a few minutes to get used to the steering and the brakes on the SUV. Everything was so precise, so exact and the complete opposite of Annabelle, who kind of floated back and forth across the road.

Gloria quickly discovered if she jerked the SUV's steering wheel, even a little, it overcorrected and headed for the ditch. "This is going to take some getting used to," she mumbled as she hit the brakes a little too hard and her forehead bumped the visor.

She turned onto Main Street and passed by Dot's Restaurant to the right and Belhaven's post office on the left. Gloria let out a sigh of relief when all looked normal and there were no cop cars or ambulances parked out front.

Gloria pressed lightly on the gas pedal…her plan was to circle around the block to head back to Dot's when she spotted the flashing lights straight ahead. Not only an ambulance, but also several of the Montbay County Sheriff's vehicles blocked the street in front of Nails and Knobs, Belhaven's hardware store.

Brian Sellers, Gloria's friend, owned Nails and Knobs Hardware store. A crowd of people milled about in front of the store and Gloria spotted her friend, Dot Jenkins. Dot and her husband, Ray, owned Dot's Restaurant.

Gloria veered around the police cruisers, maneuvered between a stop sign and a car parked off on the side of the street before driving into a drainage ditch and then pulling back onto the street.

The SUV easily navigated the deep ditch and narrow opening before pulling back onto the street on the other side. Gloria leaned forward and patted the dash. "Good girl. I hate to admit, but I think Annabelle would've bottomed out back there."

She quickly sped around the block and pulled into an empty spot in front of Dot's Restaurant. Gloria climbed out of the SUV and glanced in the window of the restaurant where she caught a glimpse of Rose Morris, Dot's new business partner, as she chatted with a local who was seated at a table near the front.

Gloria waved and kept going, determined to figure out what was happening down at the hardware store.

By the time Gloria arrived, the crowd outside the hardware store had grown. She eased her way past several bystanders as she searched for her friend, Dot.

Gloria's blood ran cold when she heard whispers of the words robbery and attack. She prayed a silent prayer for Brian as she continued to snake her way past the onlookers.

Finally, she spotted the top of Dot's head near the front and made her way over. "What happened?" she asked in a low voice.

Dot spun around, her eyes filled with concern. "They're saying someone robbed the hardware store and attacked Brian," she whispered. "Lucy ran over to Andrea's house to get her." Lucy was also one of Gloria's close friends.

Gloria sucked in a breath and closed her eyes, her head spinning. Who would rob a small town hardware store? It was unheard of! She hated to ask the words, but needed to know. "Is...Brian okay?"

Dot shook her head. "I have no idea. The ambulance arrived a few minutes ago. The paramedics carried a stretcher inside but so far no one has come out."

Gloria shifted her gaze and stared through the store's large picture window. She caught a glimpse of uniformed officers moving about but saw nothing else.

Suddenly, the crowd began to shuffle back as the front door opened and the paramedics, carrying a stretcher and a person, eased down the steps and to the rear of the ambulance.

"Brian!" A shrill female voice rang out. Andrea Malone pushed her way through the gawkers and darted over to the stretcher the paramedics were loading into the back of the ambulance.

Gloria sprang into action as she ran to her friend's side and addressed the paramedics. "This is the victim's fiancée. Can she ride with him to the hospital?"

One of the paramedics turned his head and glanced at Andrea. "I'm sorry ma'am. We don't allow family or...fiancée's in the back."

He finished pushing the stretcher in the narrow opening and closed the door. "We're on our way to the Green Springs Memorial Hospital if you want to meet us there."

"Of course." Gloria touched Andrea's arm. "I'll drive."

Dot and Lucy stood behind Gloria. "I'll let the others know what's going on," Dot said.

"I'll hang around here to see if I can find out what happened and also make sure police lock the place up when they're finished," Lucy offered.

"Sounds good. We'll follow the ambulance to the hospital since they won't allow Andrea to ride with Brian," Gloria explained.

Dot, Andrea and Gloria headed toward the restaurant while Lucy circled the edge of the crowd in an attempt to get closer to the hardware store's front entrance.

When the trio reached the restaurant, Gloria stopped in front of the SUV. "I'm driving this today."

Andrea nodded, climbed into the passenger seat and pulled the door shut behind her. "Where's Annabelle?"

"She wouldn't start this morning," Gloria explained. "Gus loaned me this vehicle while he looks at my car."

The brief conversation ended and Andrea stared out the passenger window. Gloria had no idea what to say so she kept quiet and prayed the entire time. She prayed for both Brian and Andrea, that they were only taking Brian to the hospital as a precautionary measure and that his injuries were minimal.

Gloria glanced at Andrea and noticed her face was pale and drawn. She couldn't imagine what was going through the poor woman's mind. "Do you want to call Alice?" Gloria asked quietly.

Andrea twisted her head. "I...no. She's not home. Mario Acosta picked her up early this morning to work at the kennel and training center."

Gloria had loaned money to *At Your Service Dog Training*, a service dog-training center, to help get the business up and running. It had taken some time to get things going but business was booming, so much so they had to add additional staff and had even expanded the boarding kennel.

Mario Acosta, the owner, had proudly informed Gloria he would be able to make the final repayment of the money she had loaned the following month.

Gloria was thrilled...thrilled for the families who received the special pets, thrilled for the animals themselves since the facility had originally operated as a puppy mill, and thrilled for the blossoming romance she noticed between Mario Acosta and Alice, Andrea's former housekeeper and current housemate.

It was a win-win situation for everyone. Everything was going along splendidly...until now. Her thoughts turned to Brian and the rumored robbery. Why the small hardware store? Why not the drugstore? Surely, a robber would know a drugstore would be a more attractive target than a place that sold nuts and bolts!

They had reached the hospital, located in downtown Green Springs. Gloria drove past the emergency room entrance and noticed an ambulance, backed up to a set of side doors. "That must be Brian's ambulance," she said.

Gloria pulled into the first empty spot she found. The women jumped out of the SUV, darted across the parking lot and strode into the emergency room.

Andrea spotted the check-in desk first and made a beeline with Gloria right behind her. "Yes. My fiancé, Brian Sellers, arrived by ambulance. Where do we go?"

The woman lowered her gaze as she tapped the computer keyboard and stared at the screen. "He must have just arrived. I don't see anyone by that name."

The woman leaned across the counter and pointed to a hallway on the other side. "Go through those doors, follow it to the end of the hall, make a right and you'll see another, smaller reception desk. They should be able to help you."

"Thank you." Gloria reached for Andrea's hand and the women headed through the doors. They followed the long hall and turned. Just as the clerk had told them, around the corner was a smaller check-in desk.

The area appeared to be a little more fast-paced and hectic than the other, larger check-in, as medical staff in scrubs darted back and forth.

Gloria scanned the room, hoping to catch a glimpse of the paramedic who had loaded Brian into the back of the ambulance.

Meanwhile, Andrea approached the desk. "Yes. My name is Andrea Malone. My fiancé, Brian Sellers, was brought here moments ago." She started to say something else, and then lost it. Her face puckered and she burst into tears, lowering her head and sobbing into her hands.

Gloria put an arm around her shoulder and turned to the man behind the desk. "We believe he may have been injured during a robbery so we have no information on his condition, the extent of his possible injuries or if he's even..." she was going to say 'alive' but the words stuck in her throat.

The young man gazed at them sympathetically before slowly standing. "I'll see what I can find out. Wait here." He rounded the desk and disappeared through a set of doors marked, "Emergency Room."

Andrea shuffled to the sliding glass doors and stood silently staring out while Gloria paced back and forth in front of the desk. It seemed like an eternity before the young clerk returned. He rounded the counter and approached the women. "Mr. Sellers has been admitted, but unfortunately, I'm uncertain of his condition."

"What..."

The young man interrupted. "You may want to contact his immediate family to let them know what is going on."

"Do we need the family's permission to find out his condition?" Gloria asked.

The man shook his head. "The doctor in charge will decide, especially if the patient is incapacitated."

"Incapacitated," Andrea gasped, her eyes blinking rapidly.

Gloria could see her friend was coming unglued again. She put an arm around her shoulders and gently tugged. "We'll call the family, but please let us know as soon as you hear anything."

"I will," he assured them and then watched as they made their way to the small sitting area off to the side.

Andrea eased into the seat and reached for her purse and phone. "I better call Brian's parents."

The previous fall, Brian's father had retired and his parents had moved to Arizona. Andrea had mentioned to Gloria she met Brian's parents before the big move and had liked them.

Gloria watched as Andrea searched her phone and pressed the send button, her fingers trembling. Thankfully, Brian's mother picked up. "Hello Mrs. Sellers...Joan. This is Andrea Malone." She sucked in a breath. "I'm at the hospital. Brian has just been admitted."

Andrea grew silent and Gloria could only imagine what was going through the woman's mind. "Yes. I'll wait."

Andrea covered the speaker. "She's going to get Brian's dad, Peter." She shifted the phone closer to her face.

"Yes. Uh. I don't know his current condition." She went on to tell the parents everything she knew, starting with the scene at the hardware store and finished by telling them she was in the hospital waiting room. "Yes. Please. Let me know if you hear anything," Andrea pleaded before disconnecting the line.

"They're calling the hospital themselves." Perhaps the parents would be able to find out more than they had. Peter Sellers had been a well-known, well-respected county prosecutor and Gloria guessed he would have connections in the small town and even the hospital.

Time dragged, and every so often Andrea would approach the counter to ask the desk clerk if he had any news. Each time, he would shake his head and tell her no.

During the wait, Gloria phoned Dot to let her know they still hadn't heard anything. After she finished the conversation and disconnected the line, she stood. "Would you like me to go to the main waiting area and grab us both a coffee?"

Andrea began to nod when a man wearing a white lab coat emerged from the doors marked "Emergency Area." He stopped at the counter to talk to the clerk and then headed their way.

"Miss Malone?" Andrea jumped to her feet. "Yes."

"I'm Doctor Cline, the emergency room doctor who has been treating Mr. Sellers, Brian." The doctor paused, as if struggling for the right words to say. "He's in a coma."

Chapter 3

Andrea began to sway. Gloria scrambled to her feet and wrapped her arms around her young friend.

"He took a bad blow to the head and hasn't regained consciousness." The doctor paused again, letting his words sink in. "We took an MRI and it shows some swelling in his brain."

"What does that mean?" Gloria asked as she kept a tight grip on Andrea, who began to tremble violently.

"It means the swelling could continue, causing seizures among other things. It's too early to tell. This is a wait and see situation." The doctor motioned them toward the emergency room doors. "He's back here if you'd like to see him for a moment."

"Yes!" Andrea said. "Please."

The women followed the doctor past the counter, through the doors and down another hall. Medical equipment lined the hall walls and Gloria glanced to the right, noticing several doors were ajar while others were wide open, the rooms empty.

They continued past an open area where curtains hung from the ceiling, a nurse's station and then the doctor abruptly stopped in front of a door on the left. "He's in here."

Doctor Cline opened the door and stepped aside as Andrea and Gloria quietly made their way into the room.

They passed by an empty bed and approached a second bed near the window. At first, Gloria didn't recognize Brian, his face a pale, ghostly white. A sterile white bandage circled the top of his head and a ventilator covered his nose and mouth.

Andrea tiptoed over to the bed. She reached out to touch the side of his face as tears slowly rolled down her cheeks. "Brian," she whispered.

Gloria stepped over to the other side, gazed at her still friend and started to pray. They stayed near his bedside for several long moments until the doctor cleared this throat, their signal the visit had ended.

Gloria walked to the door while Andrea lingered for a long moment. Gloria's heart broke at the sight of her friend's stricken face.

The doctor waited until they were in the hall before he spoke. "We are monitoring Mr. Sellers closely. You're free to wait in the family waiting room. It's on the other side of the reception desk."

"How long before you know if his condition will improve?" Gloria couldn't bear the thought of his condition worsening.

Doctor Cline shoved his hands in the pockets of his jacket. "We don't know how long it will take. It could be a day, could be a week, or it could be even longer..."

A nurse approached and the conversation ended.

Andrea and Gloria slowly walked down the hall. They stopped at the desk to ask where the family waiting room was located and learned it was on the other side of the check-in counter.

The girls found the waiting room and stepped inside. At the far end were floral patterned sofas and matching chairs. Above one of the sofas was a large flat screen television set.

In the center of the room was a round table along with several chairs. A small kitchenette was nearby, complete with microwave, small fridge, a coffee maker and sink.

Closer to the door was a cluster of vinyl chairs and directly across from where they were standing, Gloria could see another door, a restroom sign on the front.

Gloria was at a loss for words, what to say or do that would reassure Andrea that everything would be okay. "I see a coffee machine. I'll get us that cup of coffee."

Andrea didn't answer as she shuffled over to the window and gazed out. It was as if she hadn't heard Gloria and she probably hadn't. "I guess I better call Brian's parents to let them know what the doctor said."

She pulled her phone from her purse and Gloria listened as Andrea repeated what the doctor had told them. Judging by Andrea's end of the conversation, Brian's parents had already talked to the doctor.

They spoke for several more moments. "I'll see you soon." She disconnected the line and dropped the phone into her purse. "They're on their way here."

Gloria phoned Paul, who was over at his farm, sorting through the stuff stored inside the barn. In addition to passing heirlooms to the children, the couple had decided to hold a farm auction to get rid of old farming equipment Paul had stored in his massive barns.

They had discussed getting rid of Gloria's old Massey Ferguson, but when it came right down to it, just like Annabelle, she couldn't bear to part with the tractor. Paul didn't push her on it and she was relieved.

Ryan and Tyler, Gloria's grandsons, loved the old tractor. She secretly hoped one day one of them would want to take over the old farm and the tractor might come in handy. It ran like a top, even better than Annabelle did.

"How's the car?"

"Car?" Gloria's mind drew a blank. So much had happened since the last time she'd talked to her husband. "Oh! It's down at Gus's shop and I haven't heard from him yet. He gave me an almost new loaner SUV."

"That was nice of him. Are you home?" Paul asked.

"No. I'm at the hospital with Andrea." She quickly explained all that had transpired that morning, finishing with the news that Brian had suffered brain trauma and was in a coma.

Paul was silent for a moment as he digested the news. "You said you heard someone robbed the hardware store?"

Gloria shuffled over to the kitchenette and reached for a Styrofoam coffee cup. "We're not sure. Andrea and I followed the ambulance to the hospital. Lucy was going to hang around to see if she could find out what happened and then make sure the store was secure after police finished their investigation. I haven't heard from her yet."

She had a sudden thought. "Maybe you can call the Montbay County Sheriff's Station to see if they'll tell you what happened." Paul had worked for many years as a Montbay County Sheriff and had retired a few months back, but kept in touch with his former co-workers and boss. He also did side work as security detail so he got a chance to see his old friends on a regular basis.

"I'll see what I can find out," he said. "Keep me posted."

Gloria disconnected the line and then tried calling Lucy's cell phone. The call went directly to voice mail so Gloria left a message and asked her to call back.

Next, she tried Dot's cell. A harried Dot picked up after several rings. "Good heavens! What a madhouse!" she gasped. "I think every single resident of Belhaven is trying to get in here."

Gloria could envision the chaos. "What's the word on the street? Any speculation on what happened?"

"Well, Ruth said Judith Arnett stopped by the post office not long after it happened. She said her husband, Carl, had stopped at the hardware store to pick up some washers and screws and found Brian lying on the floor in a pool of blood near the cash register."

Gloria shot Andrea, who was pacing near the door, a glance. She was glad she hadn't heard that part. "So it was a robbery?"

"It looks like it," Dot said. "Look, I gotta go. Rose is running around like a chicken with her head cut off."

She quickly told her friend good-bye before slipping the phone into her purse. It was past noon and although Gloria wasn't hungry, they needed a distraction. She walked over to Andrea. "Let's go grab a bite to eat down in the cafeteria."

Andrea stopped. "I-I'm not hungry and what if Brian comes to while we're gone?"

Gloria didn't have the heart to remind her it might be hours, or worse yet, days, before Brian regained consciousness. "We'll tell the desk clerk we're going to eat and will be back shortly." She tugged on her friend's hand and Andrea let Gloria lead her out of the waiting room.

They briefly stopped by the desk and then headed to the hospital cafeteria. The cafeteria was large and modern, and completely different from the last time Gloria had been there. Inside were several food stations, including a pizza station, pasta station, grill area and they even had an area called the garden spot.

A light lunch was in order and Gloria headed to the garden spot and salad bar. She picked up a tray and set it on the counter before reaching for a salad plate.

Andrea reluctantly trailed behind. The girls each loaded their plates with lettuce, cucumber, onion, tomatoes and other goodies. At the end of the salad bar were large kettles filled with soup. There were several to choose from...minestrone, black bean and rice, as well as a hearty chicken noodle soup Gloria decided she had to try.

The women carried their food trays to an empty table near the window and settled in.

Gloria was hungrier than she'd realized and remembered that before Annabelle acted up, she'd planned to stop by Dot's for breakfast before running to nearby Green Springs to do some grocery shopping. She hadn't eaten all day.

Gloria devoured her food while Andrea picked at hers. "You need to eat. You won't do Brian one bit of good if you waste away to nothing and end up hospitalized, too."

Andrea reached for her soup. "I know. I'll try." She managed to choke down half her salad and her entire cup of minestrone before glancing at her watch. "We should get back in case Brian woke while we were gone."

The women carried their dirty dishes to the bin near the door, emptied their leftovers in the trash and placed the dishes on top.

There was no change in Brian's condition, and the day dragged on, filled with phone calls to keep the other girls updated on Brian's status.

Andrea and Gloria were allowed a few brief visits during the day, and each time, Gloria noted the look of hope in Andrea's eyes that Brian would respond to the soft words she spoke in his ear, but each time there was nothing. No eyelid flutter, no twitch of his hand or face.

Gloria also called Paul to check in and to let him know nothing had changed. She didn't dare leave her friend alone. Some of Gloria's other friends had volunteered to come by so she could take a break, but she just couldn't do it. No, she and Andrea would see this thing through. At the very least, she vowed to stay with Andrea until Brian's parents arrived.

Finally, later in the evening, Lucy phoned to say she had some news but didn't want to discuss it over the phone. Gloria told her she would let her know when she was on her way home and would try to stop by if it wasn't too late.

Brian's parents had managed to catch a late afternoon flight and had called earlier, right after they landed in Grand Rapids to let Andrea know they were on their way to pick up a rental car.

Gloria glanced at the clock in the family waiting room. It was 7:30 and Brian's parents would be arriving at the hospital at any time.

Andrea stared out the window and then spun back around. "It has been a couple hours. Do you want to check on Brian again?"

"Sure." Gloria slid out of the chair and stood. As soon as Brian's parents showed up, Gloria would head home. She secretly hoped Andrea would go with her to get some much-needed rest, but she doubted it. "Let's go."

The women shuffled out of the room, across the hall and into the now-familiar ER area. Brian's door was partially open and the girls quietly made their way inside.

Gloria waited at the end of the bed while Andrea approached the side. She grasped Brian's hand and whispered in his ear.

It was heartbreaking to watch. Andrea was desperate for something, some sign Brian would pull through.

"He squeezed my hand!" Andrea exclaimed suddenly.

Gloria took a step closer and studied him closely. "I saw his foot twitch." She ran out of the room and over to the nurse's station. "I just noticed Brian's foot twitched and he squeezed Andrea's hand!"

One of the nurses, who was seated at the desk, sprang into action as she jumped out of her chair and jogged down the hall with Gloria hot on her heels. She made her way over to the opposite side of the bed and began speaking to Brian.

Again, he responded and Gloria silently thanked God. Things began to move quickly as more hospital staff entered the room.

One of the nurses asked them to step into the hall and the girls headed out of the room. Tears streamed down Andrea's cheeks as they hovered outside the door. "I-I can't believe it." She buried her head in her hands and began sobbing.

"Oh dear Lord. Please don't tell me he's gone!" A woman's anguished voice echoed behind them. Gloria turned to see a woman who appeared to be close to her age and with the clearest blue eyes she had ever seen. It was like looking into Brian's eyes.

"He's starting to come to," Gloria said.

"Thank God." The woman burst into tears and now both Andrea and Brian's mother were bawling. A man standing behind the woman put an arm around her shoulders.

Doctor Cline, who had hurried to Brian's side when he began to respond, strode out of the room.

Mr. Sellers released his grip on his wife and faced the doctor. "We're Brian's parents. Andrea told us our son is starting to respond."

The doctor adjusted the stethoscope around his neck. "Yes. He opened his eyes a short time ago. We need a few more minutes and will call you to come in when we're finished."

Gloria led Andrea and Brian's parents to the family waiting room. The parents paced the floor while Gloria called her friends and Paul to let them know Brian was starting to come around.

It seemed like forever, but was only just under an hour before another doctor greeted them in the waiting room. He explained Brian was a real trooper and had started to speak. They had taken another MRI and the swelling had stopped, which was another good sign.

"He is having some memory issues so I'm only going to allow a brief visit while we gauge the level of memory loss he's experiencing."

They followed the doctor to Brian's room, and Gloria and Andrea stood off to one side as Brian's parents approached the bed. They spoke to their son in low voices and kept it brief.

"He can't remember what happened." Brian's mother whispered to Gloria as they stepped away from the bed.

Andrea nodded and approached the side. She reached for Brian's hand and he pulled back. She spoke a couple more words to Brian and he responded. They were talking too softly for Gloria to hear what they were saying.

Andrea slowly turned and walked away, a stricken look on her face.

"Well? What did he say?" Brian's father asked in a quiet voice.

"That he has no idea who I am," Andrea said.

Chapter 4

Gloria's jaw dropped. "At all?"

"He asked me who I was," she whispered. "I want to go home."

Peter Sellers put a light hand on Andrea's shoulder. "Brian loves you, Andrea. He'll remember. Maybe not tonight, but he'll remember."

"Go home, dear. Get some rest. We'll stay here with Brian," Joan Sellers added.

Gloria nodded. "We'll call in the morning." She tugged on Andrea's arm and the two of them made their way out of the hospital and to the SUV.

At first, Gloria couldn't find her vehicle, having completely forgotten Annabelle was in the repair shop. Finally, she remembered. "Over there," she pointed to the SUV that looked like every other vehicle in the parking lot.

On the way home, Gloria drove through a fast food drive-thru to pick up some burgers and fries, although Andrea insisted she still wasn't hungry. Not convinced and knowing that if she weren't there, Andrea probably wouldn't eat, she ordered the food and then practically had to force Andrea to eat part of her cheeseburger and a handful of fries.

After she choked down a few bites of food, Andrea called Alice, who was home waiting for her. Gloria coasted into Andrea's drive and shifted the SUV into park. They both wearily climbed out of the vehicle.

Alice met them at the door. She wrapped her arms around Andrea and the young woman sobbed her heartbreaking story to the woman who was like a mother.

Finally, Andrea's tears subsided and Gloria followed them into the kitchen where Alice had fixed a pot of tea. Gloria stayed long enough to have a cup of tea and then told them it was time to head home.

She passed Lucy's place on her way to the farm and almost stopped to find out what information her friend had on the robbery, but she was whupped. It would simply have to wait until the morning.

Gloria could see Paul inside the kitchen when she pulled the SUV into the drive. He waited for her at the door as she climbed out of the vehicle and made her way up the steps and into the house. Gloria fell into her husband's open arms.

Over several phone conversations, Paul had already heard the entire story and she was thankful for not having to tell it again. The only part he hadn't heard was the end.

Gloria released her tight grip on her husband and eased into a chair at the kitchen table. "I'm exhausted," she admitted as she ran a hand through her hair. "This has been one of the worst days I've had in a long time."

Mally, Gloria's springer spaniel, waited patiently for Gloria to settle in before she plodded over, dropped to the floor and put her head on Gloria's feet. "Did you miss me?" She reached down to pat Mally's head.

Paul pulled out the chair next to Gloria. "I called the sheriff's station earlier. There wasn't any new information and they told me what you already knew, that they believe it was a robbery and the robber hit Brian in the back of the head."

He went on. "They think a customer interrupted the robber, who panicked and escaped through the back door. Whoever it was, emptied the cash register but didn't take Brian's wallet."

Gloria stared out the kitchen window thoughtfully and then turned to Paul. "Do they know what weapon the robber used?"

"Yeah," Paul grimaced. "It was a large wrench. I won't go into detail, but I'm not surprised Brian suffered a concussion. He took a heavy blow to the back of his skull."

"What is this world coming to?" Gloria shook her head. "Maybe they should rename Belhaven, Crimehaven instead." She slowly lifted her arms above her head and stretched. "I'm whupped."

Paul nodded. "It's getting late. Why don't you go get ready for bed and I'll let Mally out for a final potty break."

Gloria nodded wearily and headed to the bathroom. She had a feeling she would need all the rest she could get.

***

Dot poured fresh coffee into Gloria's coffee cup. "Margaret is on the way and Ruth is waiting for Kenny to arrive at the post office to hold down the fort so gossip, I mean, talk about something other than the robbery until they get here."

Lucy, who was sitting next to Gloria, sipped her coffee and reached for a raspberry twist. "Are you going to take a break and join us?"

Dot rested the coffee pot on the edge of the table. "Of course." She shifted to the side and glanced behind her. "Can Rose join us, too? She might feel left out if we don't include her."

"The more the merrier," Gloria said. "She loves to talk and has been here long enough; she may have overhead something that might be useful."

"Thanks." Dot looked relieved. "I'll warn Ray and Johnnie we're having a girls meeting and they'll have to hold down the fort for a little while."

Gloria watched Dot disappear into the back and then turned to Lucy. "Paul drove to Detroit today to move his daughter, Allie, back home."

"To move in with you?" Lucy asked as she reached for a chocolate covered donut.

"Nope." Gloria shook her head. Allie had recently lost her job as an event coordinator in the town of Ann Arbor, and although she wanted to stay in the Detroit area, she'd been unable to find a comparable job, one that would earn enough to pay her bills and keep her head above water.

Defeated and with no prospects on the horizon, Paul had finally been able to talk Allie into moving back to West Michigan, and into the farmhouse Paul owned. It was the place where he and his wife had raised their children.

"So that means you won't be bouncing back and forth between his farm and yours?" Lucy asked.

Paul and Gloria had agreed that, since neither of them was willing to sell their family farms, they would split time between both. They spent two weeks at Paul's place and then two weeks at hers. So far, it had worked out, but now that Allie was moving back, Paul and Gloria agreed to stay at her farm to give Allie, and them, some space.

Allie had assured them both it was only temporary and she was already looking for a job in the area, although steady, good paying jobs were hard to find.

Margaret wandered into the restaurant and made her way over. "I didn't think you were here. Where's Annabelle?" she asked Gloria as she settled into the seat across from her.

"She died on me," Gloria said. "That reminds me. I need to stop by Gus's after I leave here to see if he has had a chance to look at Annabelle."

Ruth was the next to arrive. Actually, she nearly ran poor Pastor Nate over in her haste to reach the table. Gloria grinned as she overhead Ruth apologize for elbowing him and then promised him she would be in church on Sunday.

When she reached the table, she dropped her purse on the floor and pulled out a chair. "What did I miss?"

"Nothing, other than Annabelle is in the shop and Allie, Paul's youngest, is moving back home. We haven't discussed the robbery yet."

"Good." Ruth nodded. "We're waiting on Dot?"

"And Rose," Gloria said.

Dot and Rose, noticing that Ruth had finally arrived, hurried over and settled into the last two empty chairs. Dot eyed the almost empty plate of decadent treats. "Uh-oh. We need a refill before we get started."

"I gotcha covered. Stay where you're at." Johnnie, Rose's husband, patted Dot on the back, reached around her and slid a large plate of decadent goodies onto the table. "I'll be right back with more coffee."

"No need. I'm right behind you." Ray, Dot's husband, headed to the other side of the table with a fresh pot of coffee and began filling cups. "Now don't you gals go dragging poor Rose into your new investigation. She might not be ready for the full Garden Girls experience," he teased.

Johnnie chuckled. "Ray, you ain't seen my Rose in action. This woman gotta stick her nose into *everyone's* business. Wild horses won't keep her away from a good mystery."

Rose whacked her husband's arm and shot him a death look. "Johnnie Morris, you better be watchin' your tongue and get back to work."

Her husband rolled his eyes. "Don't say I didn't warn ya'll."

"Hm," Rose sniffed as she watched Johnnie head back to the kitchen. "Menfolk need to mind their own business."

Gloria covered her mouth to hide her grin, certain that Rose was going to add an exciting new dimension to their investigations.

Ruth shifted her attention to Gloria. "Well? Tell us everything."

"First of all, I'm concerned about Andrea." Gloria told them how she had called Andrea's cell phone first thing that morning and it had gone to voice mail so she called the house phone.

Alice answered and told her Andrea had gone to bed shortly after Gloria had left the night before and hadn't emerged from her room yet. She promised Gloria that if Andrea hadn't made an appearance within the hour, she would bust down the door and drag her out.

Gloria told the girls everything she knew and ended with how, after she'd called Andrea, she called the hospital to check on Brian's status. The receptionist couldn't give her information, but told her the family – Brian's parents - were still at the hospital.

Gloria left her phone number at the desk and the person on the other end promised to pass the message along. She was still waiting for Brian's parents to call back. "I'm praying his memory returned. Andrea is heartbroken."

"I have a home remedy for amnesia," Rose said. "Works like a charm."

"You do?" Gloria gazed at Rose.

"Yes siree. Why, I used it on my Uncle Delmore after he was kicked in the head by a mule. He spent a week wandering around, cluckin' like a chicken, thinkin' he should be livin' in a coop so I mixed up my special blend of herbs and voila!" Rose snapped her fingers. "One dose of my miracle potion and the man was in his right mind! Claimed his memory was better than it had been in fifty years!"

"You don't say," Margaret gazed at Rose skeptically.

"We'll keep it on the backburner, just in case." Dot reached for a glazed donut and looked at Lucy. "What did you find out yesterday at the hardware store?"

"Whew!" Lucy brushed a stray strand of red hair from her eyes. "It's a good thing I stayed behind to make sure the police locked up. I've never seen such a mess. Brian must have put up a good fight."

She went on to tell them how she'd overhead the police say Brian's attacker had hit him in the back of the head with a large wrench.

"Did you see the wrench?" Gloria asked.

Lucy shook her head and then pushed her half-eaten donut away. "No, but I saw a large pool of blood. It was awful."

"Do you remember anything else?" Ruth prompted.

"No. It was pure chaos. I hung around inside the store until one of the officers told me I would have to wait outside until they finished their investigation. They took forever and finally emerged with bags of stuff, evidence I suppose."

She went on. "Before they kicked me out, I noticed the cash register was wide open."

"I wonder what they found." Gloria drummed her fingers on top of the table. "I wish I could get inside the hardware store to take a look around."

"Oh, you can," Lucy said as she reached inside her purse and pulled out a set of keys. "I have the keys."

Chapter 5

Dot frowned. "Can we do that?"

"Do what?" Ruth asked.

"Break in."

"We're not breaking in," Gloria argued. "Lucy has the keys."

"We're making sure the property is secure," Rose piped up.

"I like your way of thinking," Margaret grinned and then abruptly stood. "The concerned citizens of Belhaven deserve answers and it's our duty to give them those answers."

"You sound like a politician," Ruth snickered.

Margaret punched her friend in the arm. "I'm serious."

"I'm with you." Gloria stood. "Who's going with us?"

"I am since I have the keys," Lucy said.

"I'll go," Ruth pushed her chair back. "By the way, how did you convince the police to hand over the keys?"

"Officer Joe Nelson arrived during the investigation and he told the other investigators it was okay to give them to me."

"Sounds like legitimate possession." Rose rubbed her hands together. "I can hardly wait to see the infamous Garden Girls in action!"

The only one still on the fence was Dot, who gazed at Lucy uncertainly. "Are you sure we're not breaking the law? What if Brian doesn't want us snooping around inside his store?"

"Last I knew, Brian doesn't remember us. He may not even remember he owns a hardware store. He needs us," Gloria stated matter-of-factly.

"But the police…" Dot's voice trailed off. She was fighting a battle she wasn't going to win. The girls were going with - or without - her.

"I guess," she muttered under her breath. "But if we get arrested."

"Ray will bail you out of jail." Lucy hooked her arm through Dot's arm.

"Don't be so sure about that." Ray approached the table and reached for an empty coffee cup. "Let me guess. You're going to break into Nails and Knobs to investigate."

"We're not breaking in." Lucy held up the keys. "I have the keys right here."

"Where are you fine ladies headed?" Johnnie Morris eyed his wife suspiciously.

"To run an errand," Johnnie's wife told her husband.

"Uh-huh."

"They're going to snoop around the hardware store, searching for clues," Ray said.

"Rose..." Johnnie warned.

Rose crossed her arms and stared her husband down. "There's nothing to worry about. I'll be fine. Right?" She turned to Dot.

"I'm as concerned as Ray and Johnnie," Dot confessed.

"We'll be back before you know it." Gloria steered Dot and Rose toward the door. Lucy, Margaret and Ruth followed behind as they hurried out of the restaurant.

When they reached the hardware store, they circled around back and Gloria unlatched the fence gate. The girls stepped into the fenced-in area and huddled in a tight circle near the rear entrance.

"What's the plan?" Lucy turned to Gloria, their unofficial ringleader.

Gloria was a fly-by-the-seat-of-her-pants type investigator. There wasn't a plan, but she didn't tell them that. She shifted her gaze and studied the exterior of the building. "Does anyone know roughly what time the robbery and attack took place?"

"It was early," Ruth said. "I remember seeing lights on inside the store around 7:30 when I drove by on my way to work. It couldn't have been more than an hour later I caught a glimpse of the ambulance and police cars as they sped past the post office."

"A customer found Brian," Lucy reminded them. "The hardware store doesn't open until eight."

Gloria slowly turned her head, her attention on the back gate. "So Brian unlocked the store at eight and if Ruth is correct about the timing, it means the robbery occurred between eight and eight-thirty."

She went on. "What if the robber followed Brian through the back gate and in through this rear door?"

Lucy picked up. "To avoid being seen! I wonder if he kept this back door locked." She wandered over to the back door, inserted the key and turned the knob. The door creaked as it opened.

"Wait!" Gloria held out a hand. "The door creaked. If someone were trying to sneak in the back door, wouldn't it have creaked and Brian would've heard it?"

Lucy hovered in the doorway, giving her eyes a moment to adjust to the lack of light inside the building.

Rose barged past the others, lunged forward and shoved Lucy inside. "Lordy! Don't you know you're never supposed to stand in an open doorway?"

The shove caused Lucy to lose her balance. She fell forward, barely catching herself as she gripped the side of the door. "Huh?"

"Uh. Rose is a little superstitious," Dot explained. "She thinks if you stand in a doorway, you're caught between the world of the living and death."

Rose darted across the threshold and stood next to Lucy. "See? That's the way to walk inside a building."

The girls followed Rose and Lucy inside, careful not to linger too long on the threshold lest Rose decide to drag them inside.

Ruth was the last one in and she closed the door behind them, extinguishing their only source of light.

Gloria sniffed the still air. The room smelled like a mixture of musty and metal. She took a step forward and the floorboard creaked under her weight. "It would be hard to sneak up on Brian, what with the creaky door and creaky floorboards."

She had been in the storeroom once before and vaguely remembered the layout. Gloria stumbled forward until she reached the other side of the room and the door leading to the store. Gloria reached for the doorknob.

"Wait!" Ruth hissed. "I hear something!"

Gloria held her breath and listened. She could hear a faint scuffling noise coming from somewhere overhead.

"What is that?" Rose clutched Dot's arm.

"I..." Margaret began to speak.

"Eek!" Dot shrieked and began hopping up and down. "Something just crawled across my foot!" She shoved her way past Margaret and Lucy, and ran to the door. "Let me out of here!"

Dot elbowed Gloria out of the way, yanked the door open and ran into the front of the store.

Gloria, losing her balance, stuck her hand out and grabbed the wall to steady herself. "There has to be a light switch here somewhere." She ran her hand along the wall. "There it is." She flipped the switch and bright light illuminated the room.

The girls gazed at the storeroom floor. A small field mouse hovered near the corner of a wooden shelf.

"Heavens to Betsy! This little critter?" Margaret reached down, grabbed the mouse's tail and picked him up, holding him at arm's length so the others could get a closer look.

"Margaret Hansen! Put that thing down!" Ruth shrieked.

"This?" Margaret swung the rodent toward Ruth, who bolted out of the room and joined Dot on the other side.

"Margaret," Gloria warned.

"Okay! This critter is more scared of you than you are him." She opened the back door and tossed the mouse onto the grass. "Sheesh!"

"You should wash your hands. Rodents carry diseases," Gloria told her.

"I ain't afraid of no mouse," Margaret began to sing cheerily as she breezed into the store.

Gloria, the last one to step into the store, closed the door to the storage room behind her. She focused her attention on the back of the store and shivered as she studied the cash register, the back counter and Brian's small corner cabinet space. Her eyes settled on the oak floor and a dark stain. "This must be the spot where they found poor Brian."

Her stomach tensed as she steeled her gaze away from the floor. With a look of determination in her eyes, she turned to her friends. "It's time to turn this place upside down, girls. Leave no stone unturned."

"Or in this case, leave no screw unturned," Ruth declared.

Chapter 6

Dot and Rose scoured the front section of the store. Ruth began combing the middle aisles while Lucy and Margaret meticulously inspected each of the shelves in the back. Gloria, meanwhile, began her search in the corner where the counter, cash register and coffee area were located.

Gloria lifted several coffee cups and inspected the area surrounding it. Her cheeks burned at the thought of someone attacking their friend in such a horrific manner. What was the world coming to when violence occurred in a peaceful, quaint town like Belhaven? She vowed to get to the bottom of the attack, not only for Brian and Andrea's sake, but for every single resident in their beloved town.

Violence had no place in Belhaven and Gloria hoped when the perpetrator was caught, the judge threw the book at them!

Gloria opened the refrigerator and peered inside. The small refrigerator was full of protein shakes, yogurt, a container of hummus and a Ziploc bag full of chopped vegetables. "Huh. Health nut."

She closed the refrigerator and opened the top cabinet drawer in the compact kitchen area. Inside the drawer was a small tray of silverware. Next to the silverware was a packet of paper napkins. "Nothing here," she muttered.

The second drawer contained extra coffee cups, packets of creamer, sugar and a Tupperware tub filled with coffee.

Gloria reached down and pulled open the last drawer. "Oh my!" She reached inside and pulled out a pair of knitting needles. "Well, I'll be." She shifted her gaze and studied the contents of the drawer. Skeins of yarn filled the drawer. Next to the yarn was a set of barbells.

"Is that what I think it is?" Ruth had crept up next to Gloria and gazed inside the open drawer.

She reached inside and pulled out a skein of dark blue yarn. "Brian is a closet knitter?" Ruth held the yarn in one hand and grabbed a five-pound barbell with the other. "He knits with one hand and lifts weights with the other."

Ruth juggled the yarn and barbell. "Knit one, lift two. Knit one, lift two."

Gloria shook her head and smiled. "I had no idea." The other girls had finished their search of the store and circled Ruth and Gloria.

"I don't believe I've ever met this young man," Rose commented.

"Perhaps not," Dot agreed. "I had no idea he liked knitting. I guess you never know someone unless you live with them."

"You can also live with someone and never really know them," Lucy added.

"No truer words have ever been spoken," Margaret sighed. "Well, I guess we've run into a dead end on this one. Maybe it's time to try to talk to Andrea, see if perhaps Brian had mentioned anyone hanging around, acting suspicious."

"I was thinking the exact same thing," Gloria said as she took the yarn and barbell from Ruth and placed them back inside the drawer before closing it.

The girls retraced their steps through the back storage area. Dot bolted across the storage room and ran out onto the rear yard.

"The mouse is long gone," Margaret called out after her.

Lucy was the last to leave. She closed the door behind them, turned the key in the lock, and then tugged on it to make sure it was secure.

Dot and Rose stopped by the restaurant to check in with the guys and make sure they were still managing okay. Luckily, it was in between the breakfast and lunch crowd and they told Dot and Rose they could handle the crowd for at least another hour, before the lunch bunch started to arrive.

A caravan of vehicles descended on Andrea's place and filled her driveway – Dot's van, Gloria's loaner SUV, and Margaret's SUV. Ruth, disappointed that she had to return to work, made Gloria promise she would let her know if they were able to glean any valuable information out of their young friend.

Dot and Rose had arrived first and were waiting on the front porch. Margaret, Lucy and Gloria met them there moments later.

Rose studied the massive columns that graced the front of the home. "I had no idea there were mansions in Belhaven. You say Andrea lives here all alone?"

"She lives here along with Alice, her former housekeeper," Gloria explained as she pressed the doorbell.

Gloria could hear muffled noises from the other side and suddenly the door swung open.

Alice peered out. "Oh my! Miss Gloria. You bring the whole posse with you dis time." She shifted to the side. "Come in. Come in. Miss Andrea, she not come out of her room yet."

Alice shook her head. "Mr. Brian. His parents, they call this morning and say their son still not remember Miss Andrea. I think her heart broken."

She tapped the tip of her finger against her forehead. "He no right in his head but he love Miss Andrea. I know."

She placed a fisted hand on her hip. "You go talk some sense into her."

The others unanimously agreed Gloria should be the one to try to talk to her.

"We'll wait in the sunroom." Lucy led the others to the sunroom while Alice hurried to the kitchen to fix a pot of tea and coffee for the unexpected guests.

Gloria glanced worriedly up the stairs toward the master suite wing of the house. If Alice couldn't get Andrea to respond, how was she going to? She loved Andrea like one of her own, but knew her well enough to know when Andrea had something set in her mind it was hard to change it. To put it bluntly, Andrea could be as stubborn as a mule.

"Here goes nothing," Gloria muttered under her breath as she climbed the stairs.

When she reached the double doors leading to the master suite, she lifted a hand to knock and then paused. "Lord, please give me the words to say to this poor girl, to give her hope that everything will work out, even though I have doubts myself."

Gloria sucked in a breath and rapped firmly on the door. Nothing.

She tried again, this time a little louder. "Andrea. It's me. Gloria."

She heard a muffled response from inside and waited. Gloria tried again. This time she heard Andrea loud and clear. "I want to be left alone!" The tone of Andrea's voice reminded Gloria of a petulant five-year old throwing a temper tantrum.

Gloria used her best *I'm the mother and you'll do as I say* voice. "Andrea! I'm not leaving until you open this door."

She stood there for several long moments, and was about to give up when the door opened.

Andrea peered out through the crack in the door. "I want to be left alone."

Gloria nudged her foot in the door and wiggled it back and forth, opening the door a smidgen wider. "I know you're upset because Brian can't remember you and honestly, I can't blame you, but you aren't helping yourself – or him – by holing up in your room and feeling sorry for yourself."

"What if he's pretending? What if he does remember me and this is his way of getting out of our engagement?"

"Andrea Malone. That is not the case. Someone whacked poor Brian over the head with a pipe wrench! The man is lucky he doesn't have brain damage!"

Gloria could tell her scolding was starting to sink in and the door eased open a little more.

"I guess you could be right. I'm just having a pity party," Andrea admitted.

"Can I come in?"

The door swung open and Andrea, barefoot and wearing her pajamas, her hair sticking up all over her head, stood off to the side. She turned around and waved her in. "Come on in."

Gloria quietly closed the bedroom door behind her and stepped into the room. It was a mess. Andrea's wingback chairs that faced the fireplace were nearly invisible. Layers of discarded clothes covered the armchairs and hung off the sides.

A stack of dirty dishes covered the coffee table. A dozen different shoes littered the floor. "Good heavens! This room looks like a cyclone blew through."

"I...was going to get dressed but couldn't decide what to wear so I gave up." Andrea crawled into the unmade bed and pulled the covers to her chin. "I'm thinking about moving back to New York."

Gloria marched to the side of the bed. "New York? I thought you hated New York." Andrea loved living in their small town. She had tons of friends. Not only that, Alice was there now. She couldn't up and move away!

"Think about it. I'm cursed. First Daniel dies. Then, this house starts turning up dead bodies. Now Brian. Everything I touch and everyone I love is cursed."

Gloria strode across the room. She grabbed the clothes off one of the chairs, dropped them onto the back of the second chair before dragging the chair to the side of the bed and plopping down. "What about me? You love me and I'm not cursed!"

Andrea sighed heavily. "Not yet, but wait. It'll happen. One day something awful, something really terrible will happen to you and it will be my fault!"

Gloria was about to argue that Daniel, Andrea's first husband, had been a scoundrel. His death had been a direct result of his own actions and had nothing to do with Andrea.

She was also going to point out the bodies found inside and outside Andrea's home had nothing to do with her, either. In fact, one of them had been there before Andrea had ever been born, but the look on Andrea's face was the same stubborn look Gloria knew all too well, so she tried a different tactic.

"Poor Alice. Where will she go? She has finally found happiness, and possibly the love of her life. You're going to rip the rug right out from under a woman who is like a mother to you? What will happen to her?"

This may have been a stretch since Gloria wasn't 100% certain Alice and her boss, Mario Acosta, were an item. She had sensed an attraction between the two the last couple of times she had visited the dog-training center but so far, she hadn't heard the two were an "item."

Andrea flopped down on her pillow and placed the back of her arm across her forehead. "She'll get over it," she sighed dramatically. "At least she wasn't jilted at the altar."

Gloria rolled her eyes. "You have not been jilted at the altar." She crossed her arms and leaned back in her chair. "I never pegged you for a quitter. I thought you had more pluck than that, but I guess I was wrong."

She went on. "Well, my cousin's daughter is a real estate agent. I can get her number if you're serious..." Gloria's voice trailed off.

"Just like that?" Andrea flung her hand away and bolted upright. "You're going to let me give up just like that?"

Gloria grinned and hopped out of the chair. "Much better. The other girls are waiting for us in the sunroom. I'm going to head downstairs while you get your butt out of bed and get ready. We have work to do!"

She marched to the door and turned back. "If you're not in the kitchen in twenty minutes, we're *all* coming up here for an intervention."

Gloria didn't wait for a reply as she flung the bedroom door open and strode down the hall. "That wasn't so hard, after all!" she whispered under her breath as she headed downstairs.

Chapter 7

Andrea strode into the kitchen eighteen minutes later. "I even cleaned up my mess!"

Alice clapped her hands. "Miss Gloria, the miracle worker!" She picked up a wooden spoon from the counter and waved it at Andrea. "Next time I have trouble with you, I call Miss Gloria," she threatened.

Andrea shifted her head and wandered over to the baking dish, sitting on top of the stove. She peered into the dish. "Whatcha' making?"

"Your favorite. Chicken tortilla casserole." Alice shifted her gaze. "You must all stay to eat. You can discuss the uh – case - while I finish putting this together. It will be ready before you know it." She looked at Gloria, her eyes pleading.

A wave of guilt washed over Gloria. They had never included Alice in their investigations. Not only that, this one involved her, in a roundabout way.

Her eyes slid to Rose. It wouldn't be fair to include Rose, a relative newcomer, and not include Alice, who had been around much longer. "I would love to stay and have lunch. I'm not sure of the others."

Dot made a quick call. If they ate an early lunch, Rose and she could still make it back to the restaurant in time for the lunch rush.

Alice assured them they would have plenty of time. She began assembling the casserole as the girls gathered around the counter to discuss the robbery.

They told Andrea they had searched the hardware store and were disappointed they hadn't found a single clue. Gloria was about to mention the knitting needles and yarn, but decided to remain silent. It was none of her business what Brian did in his free time. Plus, she thought it was cool that he loved knitting. Perhaps he could teach her a thing or two!

"Did Brian mention any suspicious activity recently? Anyone prowling around the store? Strange customers coming in to purchase items? Anything that, looking back, seems odd?" Gloria asked.

Andrea swirled her teabag around in her teacup. "No...not that I can think of." She took a sip. "Wait! I do remember him saying the other day some guy came into the store asking about do-it-yourself surveillance equipment. Brian told him they didn't sell surveillance equipment and he would have to go to one of the larger supply stores. He said the guy was acting a little weird. He finally left the store and then stood outside for a long time, like he was texting on his phone. Finally he left."

"Maybe he was scoping the place out," Gloria mused aloud. "Still, why the hardware store and why Brian?"

Ruth fidgeted in her chair and Gloria turned to face her friend. Ruth, along with most of the other Garden Girls, had lived in Belhaven more years than they cared to count. She knew Ruth as well as she knew her own sister, Liz. The fidgeting meant Ruth had beans to spill. "What is it Ruth?"

"What's what?" Ruth's eyes widened innocently.

"The fidgeting," Gloria said. "You're dying to say something. What is it?"

"Me?" Ruth pressed a hand to her chest.

All eyes turned to Ruth, who slapped an open palm on the counter and groaned. "I...can't. My job..."

There was more than one way to skin a cat. "You know something. Perhaps there was a piece of mail or package Brian received that you think might be a clue," Gloria guessed.

Ruth's face reddened. She nodded but refused to speak.

"This is a tight spot," Rose blurted out. "Lordy. What are we gonna do now?"

"Search Brian's house," Andrea said. "I have a spare key."

At first, Gloria was all for it, but the more she thought about it, she found slippery spots in the plan. "What if Brian's parents decide to take a break and come by the house?"

"True," Margaret said. "Unless someone can manage to keep them away until after we search the place."

The girls decided the best plan was to wait until at least the following day to search Brian's home. Hopefully, it would give him a chance to recover some of his memory and for them, figure out his parents' plan. The last thing Andrea wanted was to have Brian's parents catch her and the others inside his home while he was lying in a hospital bed.

True to her word, Alice's chicken tortilla casserole was ready in record time. She set the piping hot baking dish on top of the stove. Gloria had been too busy to notice she had also made a side dish of rice.

"This food looks delicious, Alice," Gloria said. "Thank you for sharing it with us."

The other girls thanked Alice, as well, as they loaded their plates with the spicy casserole and rice.

Gloria scooped a generous serving of rice on the side, picked up her fork and sampled a taste. It was a mixture of black beans, corn and yellow rice. She savored her bite and tasted a small piece of fresh cilantro. "This is delicious Alice. I need to get the recipe."

The girls carried their dishes to the sunroom. Dot and Rose insisted Alice have a seat while they ran back to the kitchen for a pitcher of lemonade. After they all settled in at the bistro tables, Gloria offered a prayer. "Dear Lord.

Thank you for this food. We pray that you bless it to our bodies. Lord, we also offer a special prayer for Brian. We pray You heal his body, restore his memory and You help track down the horrible person or persons who attacked him. We thank You for Your Son, our Savior, Jesus Christ and in His name we pray. Amen."

The girls echoed amen and then dug into their food. The chicken casserole was rich and creamy, and the sauce had a bite to it. Gloria couldn't put her finger on what it was. Her eyes narrowed and she gazed at Alice suspiciously. "You didn't mix your special honeymoon salsa into this dish?"

Alice shook her head and winked at Gloria. "No, Miss Gloria. I save my special recipe for married couples only."

Andrea grinned. "Yeah. I guess I'll be getting some on my wedding night." The smile quickly faded. "If there is a wedding night."

"There will be a wedding night," Lucy vowed. "We'll get to the bottom of this."

"Don't you worry, Andrea," Dot said.

"With Gloria hot on the case, we'll track down the perp," Margaret added.

"But what if he never remembers me..." Andrea fretted.

"I'll tell you what I told the others," Rose said. "I got a special herbal potion that will help Brian remember everything you ever wanted and maybe more." She set her fork on top of her empty plate. "All you gotta do is give me the word!"

"Special potion?" Andrea frowned.

"It's a special family recipe, passed down by my Great Aunt Lajaria, who was a gypsy and the most powerful and respected member of her clan." Rose wagged her finger back and forth. "Now, don't be askin' me to share what's in it.

Aunt Lajaria tole me I would be cursed if I ever shared the secret recipe."

"Join the club," Andrea mumbled under her breath.

"We could've used it on Eleanor Whittaker during our last investigation," Gloria said.

"Now, it don't taste that great. I have to admit." Rose dabbed at the corners of her mouth with her napkin. "It might be a little tricky gettin' him to drink the stuff."

"I'll keep that in mind," Andrea promised.

Dot glanced at her watch. "We better head back to the restaurant." Rose and she carried their plates to the kitchen. Before they left, they promised Andrea they would keep their eyes and ears open and let her know if they heard any tidbit of information that might be useful.

After they left, the others helped Alice and Andrea straighten up the kitchen and load the dishwasher. Lucy and Margaret were the next to head out, leaving only Gloria. "I need to stop by the house to let Mally out for a run. If you want, we can visit Brian this afternoon."

Andrea gazed out the kitchen window. "On the one hand, I want to, but on the other..."

Gloria patted her arm. "You think about it." The fact that Andrea was out of bed was a step in the right direction. She didn't want to force her to visit Brian and become despondent again if he couldn't remember.

She hugged Alice, thanked her for the delicious lunch and then headed to the SUV. On the way home, she stopped by Gus's repair shop to check on Annabelle.

Gus was in the back, working on another vehicle. Poor Annabelle, parked near the edge of the parking lot, was all alone. Gloria patted Annabelle's trunk before heading inside.

"Hi Gus," Gloria called out as she entered the shop, not wanting to scare him half to death. She hovered in the doorway leading to the back, and then remembered Rose's superstition about doorways. She took a step back.

Gus peeked around the hood of a car. "Hi Gloria." He grabbed a rag from his pocket, wiped his hands and eased his way around the car.

"I'm here to get the verdict on Annabelle."

"I figured as much." Gus shook his head. "I'm sorry Gloria, but I don't have good news."

Chapter 8

"For starters, the starter is toast." Gus grinned. "Get it? Starters, starter..."

Gloria attempted a half-hearted smile.

"Ahem." Gus cleared his throat and his expression grew serious. "While I was tinkering around underneath, I found a small leak. Looks like you need a new head gasket, along with the starter. The fuel pump is in bad shape and Annabelle is leaking a little transmission fluid, too."

"Oh dear. All of that?" she asked.

"I'm afraid so. Mary Beth is working on a quote, but it's going to set you back a few thousand bucks," he said as he looked over her shoulder at Annabelle. "She's getting up there, Gloria, and she's gonna start nickel and diming you to death. Maybe it's time to put her to rest."

Paul had said almost the exact same thing and Gloria knew he would agree with Gus, that it was time to let Annabelle retire and purchase a newer vehicle, but it was like a betrayal of a lifelong loyal friend. "Yes, if you could have Mary Beth send over an estimate, I'll talk to Paul."

Gloria jingled the SUV keys she was holding in her hand. "While you're at it, let me know how much you want for the SUV, too."

"Rides like a dream, huh," Gus said, and he was right. The SUV was nice. It was easy to drive and if she were honest with herself, she had to admit she liked how she sat a little higher in the driver's seat and had a clearer view of other cars as well as the road. The darn thing practically floated over the bumpy roads and it was good on gas, to boot.

"Yes. I hate to say it, but it's a very nice vehicle." There it was. The word. A vehicle. Not a family member like Annabelle, but a hunk of fancy metal and parts with no character or personality, no memories...

Gloria headed to the door. "Thanks, Gus. I'll give you a call after we get the quote and price." She stepped out onto the sidewalk and averted her gaze. Poor Annabelle.

Mally was waiting for Gloria at the back door, her head peeking out the window as she watched Gloria pull into the drive. She could see Mally barking her head off as she eyed the unfamiliar vehicle.

When Gloria climbed out, she stopped barking and waited anxiously for her to open the back door.

"Have at it." Gloria held the door as Mally darted past her, down the steps and ran over to her favorite tree. After a quick stop, she raced across the gravel drive and disappeared behind the barn, reappearing moments later.

Mally came to an abrupt halt near the edge of the garden and sniffed at the tomato plants before continuing her perimeter patrol.

Gloria dropped her purse on the kitchen chair and her keys on top before returning to the porch and settling into one of the rockers as she waited for Mally to finish her run.

She gazed at the small farm across the road. A young couple, Chris and Melody Fowler, along with their young child lived in the house. Gloria didn't know much about them. They kept mostly to themselves. Of course, Gloria and Paul were gone a lot. Perhaps with summer right around the corner, the couple would be out, working in the yard or maybe even planting a garden.

Mally came skidding around the corner of the house, gravel flying as she hit the drive and then bounded up the steps, coming to an abrupt halt in front of Gloria, her tongue hanging out of her mouth. "Well! Look at you. I wish I could bottle your energy!" She patted Mally's head and Mally flopped down on top of Gloria's feet to keep an eye out for her archenemies, the squirrels.

It was a gorgeous afternoon...too nice to head indoors so she decided to stay put and enjoy the first of many glorious late spring, early summer days. Gloria closed her eyes and listened as the birds, perched in Mally's favorite tree, chattered back and forth.

Meow. Puddles, Gloria's cat, not wanting to be left out, began howling. Gloria eased out of the chair and opened the door so Puddles could join them.

Puddles wandered to the edge of the steps. When he spotted the birds flitting back and forth on the tree branches, he began "yakking" at them, which always cracked Gloria up.

"They aren't going to fly down for a visit," Gloria warned as she settled back into her chair. Puddles finally gave up on the birds and leapt onto Gloria's lap before curling up for a nap.

She wasn't sure how long she stayed in the chair, but she was in the same spot when she watched Andrea pull into the drive and park her truck next to the SUV.

"Hi dear. I'm glad to see you've decided to leave the house," Gloria said when Andrea got close.

Andrea patted Mally's head and settled into the chair next to Gloria. "I decided that I am going to head down to the hospital. Do you want to go? I mean, you don't have to..." her voice trailed off.

On the one hand, it would have been nice to stay home and enjoy the gorgeous afternoon, maybe putter around in the garden for a little while, but the look on Andrea's face changed her mind. "I'll go with you, Andrea. Give me a minute to run inside and freshen up."

Gloria handed Puddles over to Andrea and then shuffled inside to use the bathroom and grab a couple bottled waters from the fridge.

When she returned, Mally was sprawled across Andrea's feet and Puddles was gazing up at Andrea, a look of pure adoration on his face.

"Traitors," Gloria quipped as she reached for the cat.

"I'll drive," Andrea offered. "Since you drove last time."

Gloria checked Mally and Puddles' food dishes before grabbing her purse and heading back out. Andrea was already waiting in the truck and Gloria made her way over to the passenger side.

She climbed in and reached for the seatbelt. "Let's hope Brian is doing better today."

Andrea glanced in the rearview mirror and shifted into reverse. "I talked to Brian's mom a short time ago. She said he's awake and alert, but so far still can't remember a lot of things. She said it's as if his memory stopped right around the time he moved to Belhaven. He doesn't remember owning the hardware store, the drug store or the grocery store, or that he lives in the house his grandparents left him."

She looked both ways and pulled onto the road. "He thinks he's still a circuit court judge."

Gloria automatically turned her gaze to stare out the window as they drove past Main Street and Nails and Knobs Hardware Store. She remembered Ruth's odd behavior and her suspicions that perhaps Brian had received some sort of package or mail that might be a clue.

Perhaps it wasn't a random robbery, after all. Had Brian been targeted? Who was the stranger who had come into the hardware store days earlier and asked about surveillance equipment? Brian was very perceptive. The fact that he'd mentioned the incident to Andrea was telling.

She wondered what, if any, evidence the police had found inside the hardware store and made a mental note to ask Paul if he'd had a chance to discuss the case again with any of his former co-workers.

Paul had called earlier to say Allie and he had made it safely back to the farm and were in the process of unloading her things. He promised to be home in time for dinner, and Gloria invited Allie to come over, too, which reminded Gloria she hadn't a clue what they would eat for dinner. Maybe they could order pizza...

"...Brian's house." Andrea had said something and Gloria, her mind on other things, had missed what she said.

"I'm sorry Andrea. What did you say?"

"I said I wondered if Brian's parents will want to stay at his house." Andrea patted an oversize bag next to her. "I brought some clothes and things along in case they want a break. I can let them drive my truck back to his place and they can drop you off along the way." It was apparent Andrea had given this some thought. Perhaps she thought if she could get Brian alone, she could talk to him, maybe jog his memory.

Andrea pulled into the hospital parking lot and the first empty spot she found. She shut the engine off and reached for the door handle. "Here goes nothing."

Gloria glanced around as they walked across the parking lot toward the emergency room entrance. The parking lot was full.

"He's in the same room," Andrea explained as they passed by the check-in desk and made their way to the now-familiar "family room." Several people were inside and Gloria scanned the room searching for Brian's parents. She found them seated alone, in the corner.

Andrea caught Joan's eye and the women hurried over to greet them. Joan stood and gently hugged Andrea.

"I thought you two might like to take a break. I can hang around here and keep an eye on Brian," Andrea said as she hugged her in return.

Gloria caught a glimpse of an uneasy look that passed between Brian's parents. "Is everything okay?"

"There's been no change in his condition, if that's what you're asking," Peter Sellers answered.

"Brian has a...visitor," Joan blurted out.

Chapter 9

"A visitor?" Andrea frowned. "Family?"

"An old friend," Brian's mother admitted.

Andrea's face became expressionless as she put two and two together. "An old girlfriend," she guessed and judging by the look on Brian's parents face, Gloria was certain she had hit the nail on the head.

"C'mon. Let's go see Brian." Andrea spun on her heel and stomped out of the waiting room.

Gloria tried to calm her as they walked but it was as if Andrea hadn't even heard her. They marched down the hall, their heels clicking in tandem on the gleaming hospital floor.

The door to Brian's room was open, the curtain partially drawn.

Gloria heard the tinkle of a woman's laughter from the other side. Apparently Andrea had heard it, too, as she strode across the room and flung the curtain to the side. "Who are *you?*"

A young blonde woman spun around and faced Andrea. She looked Andrea up and down, a sneer on her face. "I'm Tiffany Cartwright, Brian's friend. And who are *you?*"

The first thing Gloria noticed was the woman looked a lot like Andrea. She was a petite, attractive blonde. Andrea's eyes were a striking blue and the other woman's, a sapphire green that glittered dangerously.

"Andrea Malone. Brian's fiancée!"

The sneer never left the woman's face as she gazed at the large diamond ring on Andrea's finger. "Really?"

The woman turned her attention to Brian. "I had no idea you were engaged, Brian. When did this happen?"

Brian stared at Andrea blankly. "I...don't know. I mean. I can't remember." He rubbed his brow.

Tiffany turned and Gloria studied her face. It was a mask of ugliness. She was a good judge of character, and the first thought that popped into her mind was the woman was the epitome of the phrase "beauty is only skin deep."

She took a step forward in an attempt to diffuse a tense situation. "Brian and Andrea are engaged, but as you know, Brian was injured and is suffering from amnesia."

"Funny how Brian remembers me but not his own supposed fiancée," the woman scoffed.

Andrea had reached her boiling point as she grabbed the woman's arm and yanked her away from the bed. "Leave now before this gets ugly," she threatened.

"Ladies!" Brian jerked forward in an attempt to break up the spat. His face turned pale white.

His hand dropped to his side and he fell back in the bed, moaning under his breath.

It was that precise moment, a nurse darted into the room. "Mr. Sellers should be resting. All of you need to leave," she informed them in a stern voice.

The trio slipped out of the room, their heads lowered. Andrea was the last to leave. "I'm sorry Brian," she whispered as she shuffled out.

Gloria waited for her in the hall. She could see the woman – Tiffany – up ahead. Andrea saw her, too, and started after her.

Gloria flung her arm out, almost clotheslining Andrea. "No. You need to let this go. The last thing we need is for you two to get into a knockdown, drag out brawl and have twinkle toes there, press charges and you end up in jail."

"True." Andrea's shoulders slumped. "She's lucky I didn't deck her. Her hair was faker than she was. Did you see that? She's not even a real blonde!"

Gloria purposely walked slow, giving Andrea plenty of time to rant and rave over Brian's ex-girlfriend before they joined Brian's parents. She hoped the ex had enough sense to leave.

They stepped into the waiting room and Gloria let out the breath she was holding when she saw that Brian's ex was nowhere around.

Peter and Joan Sellers caught a glimpse and hurried over. Brian's mom touched Andrea's arm. "I'm so sorry. I-I..." her voice trailed off.

"Tiffany is strong-willed. We tried to tell her she couldn't see Brian but she ignored us and went anyway," Peter Sellers said.

"How did she know he was here?" Gloria asked.

"She read about it in the paper. After all, it's not every day a former judge is attacked, knocked unconscious and is suffering from amnesia," his mother replied.

Gloria studied Joan Seller's face. It was drawn and haggard. So was Peter Sellers' face. They both looked exhausted. "Andrea has volunteered to stay with Brian if you'd like to head over to his place to get some rest."

Joan started to say no, but Peter interrupted. "We're not doing Brian any good by wearing ourselves out. Even the doctor said he's on track to make almost a one hundred percent recovery."

"What about his memory?" Andrea asked. "Did the doctor say he'll regain his memory?"

The parents exchanged an uneasy glance.

"No. They don't know yet," Joan admitted.

"So he may never remember me," Andrea whispered.

"Even if he doesn't, he'll fall in love with you all over again." Gloria said. She wasn't sure if that was true, but she hoped it was.

"We'll go tell him we're heading to his place to get some rest and be right back." Brian's parents walked out of the waiting room and Gloria watched until they disappeared from sight.

"Are you sure you'll be okay here by yourself? What if Tiffany comes back?"

"She better not," Andrea gritted between clenched teeth. Gloria hoped not, for both of their sakes.

Brian's parents returned a short time later. They told her Brian didn't seem bothered by the fact they were leaving and Andrea was staying. "So you don't think he'll mind if I check in on him later?" she asked.

"Not at all. He seemed more upset Tiffany showed up. The two of them dated for several years and I won't go into details, but it ended badly. Brian hasn't forgotten that part," Joan said.

"In fact, Brian smiled when he told us what happened and how you were going to toss Tiffany out of the room."

Gloria hugged her young friend and turned to go when Andrea whispered in her ear. "When you get home, can you call Rose to let her know I'm willing to try her special herbal remedy on Brian?"

Chapter 10

The Sellers dropped Gloria off near her back porch. She waited until Andrea's truck disappeared down the road before heading up the porch steps. Paul was home and Gloria could see him moving back and forth in the kitchen through the window.

She stepped in the back door and spotted Allie, Paul's daughter, sitting at the kitchen table. Gloria had completely forgotten Allie was coming over for dinner. She set her purse on the chair and hugged her stepdaughter. "Well look at this beautiful ray of sunshine."

Allie grinned, the dimple in her cheek deepening as she greeted Gloria. "I hope I'm not imposing," she said.

"Not at all." Gloria made her way over to Paul, kissing her husband before turning back. "I haven't been home since early afternoon. Do you mind if we have pizza for dinner?"

"Not at all," Paul said. "In fact, I said the exact same thing. Great minds think alike."

Paul ordered the pizza while Gloria headed to the bathroom to freshen up. When she returned, Paul and Allie were sitting at the kitchen table chatting.

"I have a job interview already," Allie told Gloria as she settled into a kitchen chair. "Dad put in a good word at the Montbay County Sheriff's Department and I'm gonna meet with his old boss tomorrow."

Gloria perked up. "How exciting."

"If she lands this job, don't be getting any ideas," Paul warned.

"Ideas?" Gloria pressed a hand to her chest, her eyes wide and innocent. "Whatever do you mean?"

"You know exactly what I mean," Paul said and turned to his daughter. "It seems Gloria's sleuthing somehow always manages to involve the Montbay County Sheriff's Department."

"Not every time," Gloria argued. "Just most of the time."

Allie winked at Gloria. "Don't worry, Dad. It'll be fine."

Gloria changed the subject but in the back of her mind, she hoped Allie would get the job! She told Allie about Brian's amnesia and how Andrea and she had arrived at the hospital only to discover Brian's ex was visiting him, how he remembered Tiffany Cartwright, but still couldn't remember Andrea.

"That's a shame," Paul said. "So he still can't remember what happened?"

The pizza delivery driver arrived and the conversation paused. A thought occurred to Gloria as she watched Paul pay for the pizza. She remembered how Ruth had acted as if she knew something but couldn't tell.

They ate their pizza along with fresh, buttery breadsticks Paul had decided to order at the last minute. Not long after they finished eating, Allie told them she wanted to head back to the farm to do a little more unpacking and to get ready for her interview the next morning.

Paul and Gloria walked her to her car and then wandered to the garden so Gloria could inspect the spring plantings. In another week, it would be time to plant a few more crops, but it had been a cold, wet season so far and forecasters were predicting patches of frost for the following evening. They had had a few beautiful days, but just as many cold and rainy ones.

She had already planted some tomatoes, onions, broccoli and cauliflower, and was days away from adding corn, potatoes and watermelon. The fragile sprouts were poking up through the dark, rich soil. Gloria hoped the light frost would spare her garden.

Mally trotted along the edge of the garden, she watched Paul and Gloria closely as they inspected the crops. She knew she was not allowed in the garden, not until later in the fall after all of the crops had been harvested.

"We'll plant the corn next," Gloria told her beloved dog as she tiptoed over the top of the plants and bent down to pet her.

Paul pulled the garden hose from the reel and turned the faucet on as he started to water the plants. Gloria, meanwhile, wandered over to the grape vines growing near one of the smaller out buildings. She had planted the vines years ago as kind of a fluke.

Although it had taken a few years to start producing, Gloria was tickled every spring when they began to bud and she knew by fall, they would have a plentiful harvest.

By the time they headed back inside, it was dark. Gloria pulled a tub of butter pecan ice cream from the freezer and scooped a heaping spoonful into two bowls. Paul and Gloria carried their bowls to the living room to watch the local news and listen to the weather forecast.

After they finished the ice cream, Gloria carried the bowls to the kitchen to rinse them out and put them in the dishwasher. She reached for the light switch to turn it off when she noticed her cell phone sitting on the counter.

Gloria switched it to on and glanced at the screen. There was a message from Ruth. "Stop by the post office when you get a chance. I may have something of interest."

"Shoot! I forgot all about Ruth!" Gloria glanced at the clock above the kitchen sink. It was late...too late to call Ruth. Whatever Ruth had, it would have to wait until morning.

Chapter 11

Paul left early the next morning, right after breakfast. He told her he wanted to head back to the farm to work on repairing his ice shanty before putting it away for the year. The winter had been especially brutal and part of the metal roof had come loose after the wind got hold of it.

He hadn't said it, but Gloria suspected he also wanted to check on Allie, to make sure she didn't need anything. Paul's farm was out in the country, surrounded by farm fields and on the isolated side.

Gloria knew he was worried about his daughter being out there all by herself. She had offered to let Mally stay with her for a few days, but Allie insisted she was fine and wasn't afraid to be alone.

Gloria quickly finished her chores and was anxious to head into town to find out what information Ruth might have that would help figure out who had attacked Brian. She also planned to stop by Dot's Restaurant to let Rose know that Andrea was ready for Rose's special "memory enhancing" herbal concoction, which reminded her she needed to call Andrea to see if Brian's condition had changed.

Gloria's call went right to voice mail and Gloria left a message on Andrea's cell phone before she hopped in the shower. The morning forecast called for cool temperatures and heavy cloud cover, giving way to afternoon sunshine. Except for the threat of the light frost that night, the weather was finally starting to improve.

Paul had taken Mally with him to the farm. Gloria knew her pooch would have a ball running around the farm, keeping Paul company for the day and helping repair the shanty.

She checked her email before heading out in hopes Mary Beth had a chance to send over the estimate to repair Annabelle but there was nothing from Gus or Mary Beth.

Gloria hopped into the SUV and headed toward town. She almost stopped at Gus's shop, but didn't want to seem pushy about the quote so she drove past.

When she reached Main Street, Gloria pulled into the post office parking lot and a spot near the street. She reached for her purse and grabbed the door handle when her cell phone began to ring. It was Andrea.

"Hello dear. How's it going?"

Andrea let out an aggravated sigh. "No change. Brian and I had a long talk before he went to bed last night, but he still doesn't remember anything...or me."

"I just pulled into the post office. I'm going to chat with Ruth for a minute and then head over to Dot's Restaurant to talk to Rose about the memory miracle cure she told us about, if you're still interested."

"Yes!" Andrea said. "Brian is getting antsy and bugging the doctor about being released. The doctor said he might discharge Brian later today or tomorrow. We'll need to get him to try the potion before he goes home. I think it will be easier to get him to try it if he's trapped in a hospital bed."

"What about Brian's parents?" Gloria asked.

"That's another thing," Andrea said. "They had some errands to run this morning, but plan to be back here around one o'clock. We're going to switch shifts again. If they release him from the hospital later today, our chance to give him Rose's miracle cure might be lost."

It was already nine in the morning. They only had a few hours! "Oh dear. I'll try to get Rose and/or the potion there by eleven." She quickly disconnected the line, climbed out of the vehicle and headed toward the front door of the post office.

Ruth was behind the counter, waiting on a customer. When she caught a glimpse of Gloria walking through the front door, she abruptly cut the customer off.

As soon as the woman left the post office, Gloria approached the counter.

"Remember when I said I might have something?" Ruth reached behind the counter, pulled out a small stack of envelopes and slid them toward Gloria. "These have been coming in for about a week now. At first, I didn't think too much about it, but this might be a clue."

Gloria reached inside her purse, pulled out her reading glasses and slipped them on as she lifted the envelope on top:

"Nails and Knobs Hardware Store

Attn: Hiring Manager

832 Main Street

Belhaven, Michigan 49505"

Gloria set the envelope to the side and read the second, then the third. There were four envelopes in all, and all of them addressed to the hiring manager. "So Brian placed a help wanted ad for the hardware store." She tapped the tip of the envelope against the palm of her hand. "Interesting."

Gloria placed the envelope on top and slid them across the counter. "Perhaps someone showed up the other morning, posing as a potential employee, but instead robbed the store."

She went on. "When I get home later, I'll look through the last few days' newspapers to see if I can find Brian's ad."

"Or check the newspaper on line," Ruth suggested.

"Good idea!"

"How is Brian doing?" Ruth asked.

"I just talked to Andrea. He knows his parents, even remembers an ex-girlfriend, but still can't remember he owns businesses and lives in Belhaven or that Andrea and he are engaged."

Ruth tsk-tsked. "Such a shame. I hope he remembers by August."

Andrea and Brian had picked August 12th for their wedding date. Margaret had offered to let them use her backyard for the wedding ceremony since they had the perfect set up and a big, beautiful covered dock leading out to the lake.

The plan was for Pastor Nate to marry them on the dock, and then have the reception at Andrea's spacious home. The plans even included a makeshift dancefloor set up in the sunroom.

The reception would be similar to the one Gloria and Paul had had at Andrea's place the previous December, but on a much larger scale. All of the Garden Girls were helping Andrea with the arrangements and it promised to be the event of the season!

"I hope he remembers, too, which reminds me I need to run across the street to talk to Rose about her special potion to restore Brian's memory."

Ruth wrinkled her nose. "I hope it works."

"Me too. We have to convince him to try it today, though. Andrea said the doctor might release Brian from the hospital later today or tomorrow and then we won't have a chance to slip him the potion."

"Sounds exciting," Ruth groaned. "How come I always have to miss out on all the fun?"

"Sorry Ruth. We would wait for you if we could." Gloria slipped out of the post office and headed across the street. Dot's Restaurant was filled with customers and Gloria headed to the back.

It was all hands on deck as Ray, Dot, Rose and Johnnie darted back and forth between the kitchen and the server area.

Dot noticed Gloria first. "Hi Gloria! This place is a madhouse this morning!"

Rose reached for a breakfast plate filled with a heaping mound of scrambled eggs, crispy slices of bacon and a small stack of wheat toast. She set it on her tray and grabbed a second plate piled high with blueberry pancakes. "Be right back."

She headed to the dining room with Dot right behind her, coffee pot in hand. The girls returned several minutes later and Rose slid her empty tray onto the top of the pass thru window. "How's that young man, Brian?"

"That's why I'm here. He still can't remember Andrea or the fact he owns half of Belhaven. Andrea is getting desperate and wants to know if you can whip up a batch of your special memory potion."

Rose grinned from ear to ear. "Girlfriend, I had a feeling she was gonna want it so I went ahead and mixed a batch." She lowered her voice and glanced around. "But we need to keep it on the down low. Johnnie, he don't like me makin' this stuff. He thinks it's dangerous."

"Be right back." Rose darted across the server station and disappeared in the back. She returned moments later with a small vial of amber-colored liquid. Rose handed it to Gloria.

"Why does Johnnie think it's dangerous?" Gloria asked as she took the vial.

"Well. Now, this has only happened once or twice, but I mixed it a teeny bit too strong." Rose pinched her index finger and thumb together and then separated it, just a tad. "I gave it to Johnnie's sister, Melody, or Mel as we call her. She took too much of it and Lordy! The woman would not shut up. Why she talked nonstop for three days and that is no exaggeration. She told story after story about Johnnie growing up and how much trouble he got into."

Rose rolled her eyes. "Whew! He was spittin' mad. Why, I had to quick whip up another potion in order to calm motor mouth Mel down." She shook her head. "Which reminds me. Make sure you put only two small drops into his drink.

The potion has a strong odor so try to use somethin' to disguise the smell...and taste."

Gloria held up the bottle. "May I?"

"Oh, sure. Have a whiff, but not too close," Rose warned.

Gloria slowly unscrewed the cap and lifted the vial. The overpowering stench of roadkill, rotting eggs and a third odor she couldn't put her finger on assaulted her nostrils. Her hand flew to her mouth and she swallowed hard, her stomach churning. "Oh my gosh! That's awful."

Rose glanced behind her. "Shhh! Johnnie is right over there."

Gloria quickly screwed the cap back on and slipped it into her purse. "What's in that?"

"Eastern skunk cabbage, ground bombardier beetle and a couple other herbs." Rose waved a hand. "I can't share the rest. Remember how I told you about Great Aunt Lajaria and the curse?

I added my own special ingredient...ground up stems from forget-me-not flowers."

She went on. "Remember...don't give him too much. A couple drops will do."

"How long will it take before we'll know if it works?" Gloria asked as she snapped the clasp on the front of her purse.

"With Mel it worked right away, but with Uncle Delmore, it took a little longer. Maybe a day."

Gloria thanked Rose for the potion, stopped by to chat with Dot and then headed out. She wanted to get to Andrea...and Brian, before Brian's parents returned to the hospital. She climbed into the SUV and offered up a small prayer Rose's stinky potion would do the trick.

Chapter 12

Andrea jerked her head back and pinched her nose. "Oh my gosh! That smells so bad," she gasped.

"I tried to warn you. I think it singed my nose hairs. I can still smell it," Gloria said. "We have to figure out what to mix it with so Brian will actually get enough in his system for it to work."

The girls stepped over to the vending machine sitting in the corner of the waiting room and studied the canned beverages on display.

Andrea went down the line. "Coke won't work. Sprite definitely won't work."

"What about root beer?" Gloria asked.

"Brian hates root beer."

"Orange juice!" Andrea exclaimed. "It might mask the taste, plus Brian loves orange juice."

She slipped two one-dollar bills into the machine and pressed the button. The small can of orange juice dropped into the tray at the bottom of the machine and Andrea fished it out. "Should we add ice before we pour it in a glass?"

"Rose said he needs to ingest two drops. The more we water it down, the less he'll swallow, unless he drinks it all."

"We'll skip the ice," Andrea decided.

The women made their way over to the coffee station. Gloria pulled a Styrofoam coffee cup from the stack and Andrea dumped the container of orange juice into the cup.

Next, Gloria unscrewed the cap on the potion, tipped the vial to the side and carefully squirted two drops of Rose's potion into the cup. She grabbed a stir stick and swirled it around.

"Here goes nothing." Andrea led the way and Gloria followed behind, holding the cup in her hand, careful not to slosh the contents over the sides of the cup.

When they reached Brian's room, he was sitting up in bed, watching television. He smiled and set the remote next to him when they entered the room. "The doctor will be by in another hour or so to let me know if they're going to spring me from this joint."

"That's wonderful." Andrea tiptoed to the side and Gloria stepped closer to the bed. A flicker of recognition flashed across Brian's face. "I..." he snapped his fingers. "You're..."

"Yes..." Gloria leaned forward.

"Ugh! It's on the tip of my tongue. The nosy lady, Ginger!"

Andrea giggled.

Gloria frowned and shook her head.

"Here, I brought you some orange juice." Andrea held out the cup.

Brian stared at the cup she was holding. "Do I like orange juice?"

"You love orange juice," Andrea replied.

Brian took the cup from her and put it to his lips before wrinkling his nose. "This smells funny." He took a small sip and held it out. "Yuck. I think the orange juice expired. Here. Taste it."

Andrea took the cup, a deer-in-the-headlights look on her face. She lifted the cup and pretended to sip. "I...don't taste anything wrong with it."

Brian frowned. "What about the nasty smell?"

Right then, the nurse entered the room, followed by the doctor.

Gloria's heart sank. The mission had been a failure! Andrea, cup in hand, shuffled out the door and hovered in the hall.

Gloria followed her out. "Maybe we should just tell him..."

"Tell him what?" Andrea interrupted. "That we're giving him some voodoo potion a woman he doesn't even know made for him in hopes he'll remember? He's already suspicious since he can't remember any of us."

"There has to be another way." She began to pace back and forth.

Gloria took the cup from Andrea's hand and studied it thoughtfully.

The doctor, accompanied by the nurse, emerged from his room. "He wasn't very happy about that," the nurse murmured to the doctor as they walked past.

"They must be keeping him another night," Andrea whispered.

It was bad news for Brian, but good news for Andrea and Gloria. Perhaps they would have another opportunity to try to get him to drink Rose's potion.

"There you are!" Andrea spun around and came face to face with Joan and Peter Sellers. "I'm sorry if we're late."

"Oh no. You're fine," Andrea assured them.

While Andrea chatted, Gloria looked around for a place to dispose of the tainted orange juice. She hurried over to a nearby drinking fountain and dumped the contents down the drain, rinsed the cup and tossed it in the nearby trashcan.

"...and if you don't mind. We ran into the doctor a moment ago. Brian will have to stay one more night. They're going to release him tomorrow morning. I'm sure he's less than thrilled," Joan Sellers told Andrea.

"We'll spend the rest of the day with him, but wondered, if it isn't too much to ask, if you could take one more night shift," Peter Sellers said. "My sister, who lives in Detroit, is driving over to see us and she'll be here a little later."

"Of course," Andrea said. "I don't mind at all." She stepped into Brian's room to tell him she would return later that evening and then made her way back to the hall to say good-bye to Brian's parents. She wasn't smiling. "He asked me why I keep hanging around. He said he appreciated it and everything, but he looked at me like he thought I was crazy." A lone tear trickled down Andrea's cheek. "I hope he remembers me soon."

"He will, Andrea. Don't worry." Brian's mom put her arms around Andrea and held her close. "Give him time dear. He'll remember."

Andrea dabbed at the corner of her eye while Gloria slipped her arm through her young friend's arm, and the two of them headed out of the hospital and to the SUV.

Andrea's truck was parked close to the entrance and not far from Gloria's SUV. "I can take my truck home so you don't have to drive back later."

"Okay." Gloria gazed back at the hospital. "There has to be some way to get Brian to down two drops of the potion. Let me think about it. I'll call you later." She gave Andrea a quick hug and then headed to her vehicle. She clicked the key FOB and opened the driver's side door.

Gloria waited for Andrea to drive out of the parking lot before backing out of her parking space. She had completely forgotten to ask Andrea if Brian had been running an ad for help at the hardware store and made a mental note to ask her later.

She followed Andrea as far as Main Street in Belhaven. While Andrea continued past the stop sign toward home, Gloria pulled into a parking space in front of the restaurant and climbed out of the car.

The lunch crunch had ended and she could see Dot and Rose standing near the cash register. Rose rushed over when Gloria stepped inside. "Well? Did it work?"

"Nope. We mixed it with some orange juice. Brian took one whiff of the juice, thought it had expired and refused to drink it."

Rose's face fell. "I need to work on improving the smell. It has always been my downfall."

Johnnie, Rose's husband, walked over. "Two visits in one day, Gloria. What's the occasion?"

Gloria gave Rose a quick glance and Rose shook her head.

"I-uh. Was just giving Rose...and Dot an update on our friend, Brian."

"Terrible tragedy." Johnnie shook his head. "I wouldn't expect such a violent robbery in a town like Belhaven. What's this world coming to?"

Dot strolled over. "Any news on Brian?"

"No change. Nothing is jogging his memory." Gloria gave Dot a meaningful stare. "They're going to release him from the hospital tomorrow morning. Andrea is heading back over there this evening."

"I think we should visit him this evening," Rose blurted out. "Why, perhaps one of us can jog his memory."

"He has never even met you." Johnnie shifted his gaze and stared at his wife. "You're not thinking of giving that poor boy your hocus pocus potion…"

Rose clasped her hands and batted her eyes. "Me? Why Johnnie, you know I gave up on my potions when Sadie Benson took too much and had that unfortunate reaction."

Gloria leaned forward, curious to hear about Sadie. "What happened to Sadie?"

Johnnie tipped back his head and laughed. "Sadie was our neighbor back in Georgia. She was startin' to show signs of dementia. Rose, here, talked Sadie into trying her memory potion. Next thing I know, poor Sadie thinks she's an exotic dancer. Why, we couldn't get her to keep her clothes on! The woman was ninety-five years old!"

Gloria turned to Rose, a horrified expression on her face. "You're kidding."

"I had to tweak the potion, plus she took way too much. It was her fault. She recovered," Rose finished lamely.

Johnnie made his way to the back and Gloria waited until he was out of earshot. "I don't know about this Rose. What if we're able to get Brian to take the concoction and nothing happens? Or worse yet, he thinks he's a stripper?" Vision of Brian running up and down the hospital corridors naked as a jaybird flashed through Gloria's mind.

The nurses would be thrilled, but Andrea? Not so much. She might never forgive them!

"I promise. I have the levels just right," Rose assured her. "If we can get him to take a couple drops, he'll be back to his old self, he will remember everything and most important, he'll remember his beloved bride-to-be."

Rose's declaration tugged at Gloria's softer side and she caved. "Okay, but if this goes bad, I'll never forgive myself...or you." She gave Rose a pointed stare.

"I promise," Rose replied in a small voice. "Cross my heart." She made an "x" across her chest.

"I'm still not convinced," Dot said. "How many times have you tried this potion and how many times has there been a problem?" Dot was determined to pin Rose down.

"Well." Rose clasped her hands and began twisting her fingers. "There was Uncle Delmore."

"Who thought he was a chicken," Gloria said.

"Then there was Melody, Mel, Johnnie's sister," Rose said.

"Who talked nonstop for days," Dot said.

"And...then there was Sadie," Rose finished.

"Who thought she was a twenty-five year old stripper," Gloria said. "Have you had one single person who took the potion and didn't have an adverse side effect?"

"Me," Rose said. "I took it once and nothing happened."

Dot groaned and rolled her eyes. "That you're aware of!"

Rose waved her hands. "Well! All side effects aside, this stuff works," she insisted. "And I have an idea on how we can get your friend, Brian, to take it. What time is Andrea supposed to head back to the hospital?"

Gloria phoned Andrea on the way home to tell her Rose had another idea on how to get Brian to take her special potion. Andrea answered on the first ring, her voice muffled. "Hang on. I'm going outside."

Gloria could hear rustling in the background, as if Andrea were on the move. "I'm glad Rose has an idea, but Houston, we have a problem!"

Chapter 13

"What...kind of problem?" Gloria asked. Perhaps they were releasing Brian from the hospital after all.

"It's Alice. She's fit to be tied, going on and on about Rose's special memory brew. She's upset because we didn't consult her first. Whew! She blew up like a nuclear bomb, ranting and raving, using Spanish words I don't know and probably don't want to know."

Andrea went on. "She has finally calmed down but she's in the kitchen, mumbling under her breath and brewing a batch of something that smells to the high heavens."

"Worse than Rose's mix?" Gloria couldn't imagine anything smelling worse than Rose's concoction.

"Well, it depends on what you mean by worse. Let's just say it's burning my eyes. She's insisting that she go with me to the hospital and that *her* special potion will work and Brian's memory will come flooding back as soon as he takes a sip."

All things being equal, Alice did have a better track record for her special mixtures working accurately. She remembered the special salsa Alice had given her and how it had worked on Paul.

Gloria turned into her drive, parked the SUV in front of the garage and shut the engine off. "What are we going to do?"

She had already told Rose she could come and there was no way she was going to tell Alice that she couldn't. It was apparent Alice thought Rose was invading her "turf." Gloria hadn't considered how Alice might be upset over Rose's attempt to help.

"I say we let them both come to the hospital. I already asked Alice how she planned to get Brian to try her spicy concoction and she told me she was gonna march right in his room and tell him she was never going to fix his favorite spicy fish tacos again if he didn't."

"Did you point out to Alice that Brian doesn't remember her, either?" Gloria asked.

"I tried, truly I did, but once Alice gets her mind set on something, there's no changing it. She's going and there's no stopping her."

Gloria attempted to reassure Andrea it would be fine, how Rose would have to understand Alice was like family and Brian held a special place in her heart.

As she hung up the phone, she wondered if any of the other girls would like to make the trek to the hospital under the guise of "visiting" Brian. She had a feeling it would be most, if not all, of them. It promised to be an exciting evening...

Gloria wandered into the house, and dropped the keys on the hook near the door and her purse on the chair. Mally made her way across the kitchen and plopped down in front of her. Not blinking. Gloria knew the look all too well. "Let me guess. You want to go out." It was turning out to be a beautiful day...a beautiful day for a nice long walk. "You want to go back to the creek?"

Gloria had only been back there once this year. Spring was slow in coming and the fields, which had been wet and mucky, were a mess. Finally, they were starting to dry out.

Mally scrambled to her feet and thumped her tail against the kitchen door.

"I'll take that as a yes." Gloria changed from her flats to her barn boots, grabbed a light jacket and they headed outside with Mally racing ahead.

Paul hadn't accompanied Gloria to the woods and creek, although she had invited him. She had a sneaky suspicion he felt he would be intruding on her "alone" time, which she appreciated, and perhaps he was right.

Her walks with Mally were a time to reflect, to ponder life's problems, which usually involved some sort of mystery.

Gloria skirted the edge of the garden and made her way between the farm fields. It was too early to tell what crops the farmers had planted.

A stiff gust of cool air barreled through the field and Gloria shivered as she slipped her jacket on, pulling it tight.

She picked up the pace and when she reached the edge of the field and the tree line, the wind died down.

Mally and Gloria stepped into the woods, zigzagging back and forth around the trees as they made their way to the creek.

Mally trotted to the edge, lowered her head and drank from the cool, clear water. Gloria settled in on a fallen tree, "her" tree. It had been there for years and it was the perfect spot to take a break and mull over the recent developments.

On the one hand, the girls could just let Mother Nature run its course. The doctor had said there was a good chance Brian would completely recover his memory. Still, there was no guarantee.

On the other hand, if Alice...or Rose's special potion actually worked, it could help move things along. Andrea seemed anxious for Brian to remember her, not that Gloria could blame her, especially with the ex-girlfriend hanging around.

There was also the upcoming engagement party. Would they have to postpone it? How could Andrea move forward with wedding plans if the soon-to-be-groom had no idea who she was?

Mally frolicked in the frigid water and then trotted over to Gloria.

"You're all wet." Gloria frowned.

It was as if Mally understood Gloria's comment and proceeded to do the "doggy shake," pelting her with droplets of cold water.

Gloria jerked her head and squeezed her eyes shut. "Mally!" She abruptly stood and wiped the water off her face with the back of her hand. "We better head back. I have to find out if Mary Beth sent the quote to fix Annabelle." She also wanted to do a little research to find out if Brian had placed an ad in the paper for help at the hardware store. So far, they had no leads and no suspects in the robbery.

Gloria was chomping at the bit to track down the robber. Until they uncovered the criminal, no one was safe!

Mally galloped ahead and Gloria followed behind, slowly retracing her steps. She caught up to her beloved pooch near the edge of the garden. Ever since Gloria had told her she had to stay out of the garden, Mally seemed drawn to it even more. She was a good dog and had obeyed Gloria's orders, although Gloria knew she didn't want to.

When she reached the porch, she found a note tucked in the door. Gloria unfolded the note and stared at the piece of paper. Without her reading glasses, she couldn't make hide nor hair of what it said.

Gloria opened the door and waited for Mally to dash past before she followed her in and closed the door behind them. She reached into her purse, pulled out her glasses and slipped them on.

"Hi Mom. The boys and I were out running errands, drove by and thought we would stop. I guess you're not home since Annabelle isn't here. Sorry we missed you. Call me later. Love you."

Gloria folded the note. "Shoot Mally! We missed Jill and the boys!" Gloria hadn't seen her grandsons for several weeks, although that would change soon since summer vacation was right around the corner. "We should see if the boys want to come spend the night."

She started for the house phone and then stopped in her tracks. It wasn't just her anymore. She would have to check with Paul to make sure he hadn't made plans for them and if he was okay with the boys spending the night. They could be a little rambunctious.

Gloria decided to postpone the call and instead headed to her desk in the dining room. First things first, she opened her email and spotted one from Mary Beth. "Here goes nothing." Gloria sucked in a breath and clicked on the quote Mary Beth had sent.

Gus had warned Gloria that Annabelle needed major repairs. She blew air through thinned lips as she scanned the quote. Gloria had no idea it would cost over three thousand dollars for the repairs. She couldn't make heads or tails of the mumbo jumbo and closed the email. Paul would have to look at it later, but Gloria knew what was coming.

He would tell her to retire Annabelle and buy a newer vehicle. Gloria shifted her gaze and stared out the front window. It would be nice to have a newer, dependable vehicle, although Annabelle had been dependable!

Gloria was leaning toward repairing Annabelle despite the hefty repair bill, but again, now that she was married, it would have to be a joint decision.

She pushed the worries over Annabelle to the side and finished reading her emails, which were mostly junk. There was one from her son, Ben, in Texas. He had invited Gloria, and Paul, to visit them in Houston since they wouldn't be able to squeeze in a visit to Michigan during the summer.

Gloria's list of things to discuss with Paul was growing by the minute – Annabelle, Tyler and Ryan spending the night, now a visit to Houston...

It was time to do a little digging. Gloria clicked out of her email account and clicked on the Green Springs Gazette's online newspaper. She typed the words, "Nails and Knobs" in the search bar and hit the return key. An ad popped up moments later:

"Small town opportunity with big time advancement. Nails and Knobs Hardware Store is looking for a unique individual to work alongside the owner, learning the business from the ground up.

Our business is growing and we're looking for the right individual to grow right along with it. If you're self-motivated, hard-working, dependable and determined, please send your resume to the following address:"

It listed Brian's hardware store address, the same address that was on the envelopes Ruth had shown her. Could it be someone who had applied for the job attacked Brian and robbed him?

She needed to find out who had scheduled a face-to-face interview with Brian. He must have had some sort of file, or notes on who he had contacted for an interview. She knew one thing for sure. Wherever he kept the information, it wasn't at the hardware store!

Gloria clicked out of the classified ads and started to click out of the *Green Springs Gazette* when something caught her eye.

"Twice convicted felon, Walter Tompkins, escapes from nearby Cascade Federal Correctional Institution."

Chapter 14

Gloria adjusted her glasses and began reading the article. The story told how Walter Tompkins, a former resident of the Grand Rapids area, along with another prison inmate, Bart Zagorski, from the Detroit area, had escaped. They were prison inmates who shared a cell and had overpowered a security guard by striking him in the head with a chunk of their metal bed frame they had managed to remove.

They had escaped from the federal correctional institute the previous week. Both men were serving time for armed robbery. Tompkins was also serving time for attempted murder.

The men had been returning to their cells after eating dinner when the incident occurred. After the men struck a security guard over the head, they held him hostage and demanded that they be released.

Authorities believed the inmates planned the attack since a car, described as a late model, possibly black, four-door sedan, had been waiting outside.

Police warned the men were considered armed and dangerous, and there was a manhunt in both Kent County and the Detroit area, as police believed the men would attempt to contact family members.

Gloria finished reading the article. Armed robbery...attempted murder. Gloria hovered the mouse over the newspaper's search bar and then typed in Walter Tompkins' name. There were several, older articles detailing Mr. Tompkins' illustrious life as a criminal. It appeared he had been in and out of trouble from a young age.

Gloria read each of the articles, and several articles in, she found what she was looking for...Brian, a former circuit court judge, had reviewed an appeal by Mr. Tompkins, who insisted he had been framed and was not the armed robber the victims had pointed out.

Brian had upheld the original court's ruling and Mr. Tompkins was returned to prison to finish his sentence. That was a few years back.

Gloria headed to her purse and her cell phone to call Andrea. The call went right to voice mail and Gloria left a message, asking her young friend to call back as soon as possible. She started to set the phone down when it began ringing.

"I'm sorry Gloria. I just missed your call," Andrea said.

"No worries dear. I'm sure you have your hands full over there. How is Alice's...special mixture working out?"

"Ugh! I had to open every window in the house. It smells like a hot sauce factory in here."

Gloria chuckled at the thought of Andrea flinging every window open. "I was on my computer and ran across an article about an escaped convict by the name of Walter Tompkins. It appears Brian may have reviewed this man's appeal case some time ago. Years ago, actually, and sided with the lower courts, sending him back to prison to complete his sentence."

Andrea cut her off. "So you think this guy Brian sent to prison and who recently escaped, came after him?"

"Revenge," Gloria said. "I wonder how hard it would be to find Brian." She didn't want to come right out and tell Andrea how Ruth had shown her Brian's mail and they discovered Brian was looking for help at the hardware store.

"I typed in Nails and Knobs" in the same online newspaper and discovered Brian had placed a 'help wanted' ad."

Andrea gasped. "You're right. He did. With everything going on, it completely slipped my mind. Do you think this Walter fellow was looking for Brian, found his name on the internet and then pretended to apply for a job?"

It was a stretch, but anything was possible. "Either that or the guy tracked Brian down from the ad and then just showed up at the hardware store, caught him off guard and attacked him."

"Or maybe it was one of the people he interviewed. When I talked to him the other night – when he still knew who I was and that he loved me – the old Brian, he told me he was lining up interviews."

"So maybe it wasn't the escaped convict after all, but another person who posed as someone interested in a job," Gloria said. "Is there any way to find out who may have been meeting Brian for the interview?"

"Yes!" Andrea said excitedly. "There is! Brian kept everything on his iPad, but I liked to tease him because he also kept a calendar book. He said he kept both in case he lost everything online."

Gloria began to pace the kitchen floor. Finally! They were getting somewhere!

"He keeps it in his home office as kind of a backup. Hang on." Andrea covered the phone and began talking to Alice.

"I'm back. The natives are getting restless," Andrea groaned. "I'm not sure what happened to Brian's iPad. It might be at the house, too."

"We should tell Brian that when he gets home he needs to search his black book. Maybe it will jog his memory," Gloria said.

The girls talked for a few more minutes, working out the details of the upcoming hospital visit. They decided that Gloria would pick up Lucy, Dot and Rose while Andrea would drive to the hospital with Alice.

Margaret had been disappointed she couldn't join them at the hospital and Ruth couldn't either, which may have been a good thing. If Brian couldn't remember any of them, it would seem suspicious if all of them descended on him at once.

Andrea told Gloria that Alice and she would go in first with the rest heading to the hospital a short time later, after Brian's parents had left for the evening. Andrea had promised Alice she could try her "memory enhancing" brew before Rose got another shot at it.

Paul arrived late afternoon and seemed disappointed Gloria was heading to the hospital again. Gloria felt a twinge of guilt at leaving him again and promised they would spend the following day together, taking in an afternoon movie matinee and then dinner afterward.

Gloria warmed leftover meatloaf and microwaved a couple potatoes while Paul set the table. "Mary Beth, Gus's wife, sent over an estimate for Annabelle's repairs. It's going to be a few thousand dollars."

Paul paused and then set the napkin next to one of the dinner plates. "What do you think?"

Paul knew how attached his wife was to the car. He had decided he wouldn't decide. He would leave it up to her. It was her car and her decision.

Gloria set the plate of piping hot meat loaf slices on the table. "I'm torn. On the one hand, it would be nice to have something newer and dependable, not that Annabelle wasn't dependable. On the other hand, Annabelle is like family..." her voice trailed off.

"I'm going to let you decide." Paul placed the second napkin next to his plate and stepped over to his wife, putting his arms around her and pulling her close. "At least I know if I start to fall apart and cost money, you won't put me out to pasture," he teased. "Or at the very least, you'll think about it first."

Gloria pulled away and whacked his arm. "Of course not!" she grinned. "Unless you don't behave." She wrapped her arms around his neck and pulled him close.

For a few moments, the newlyweds forgot about Annabelle, forgot about dinner...

Finally, Paul pulled back. "Better watch it or we won't eat dinner at all."

"That would be fine with me," Gloria shot back.

The timer on the microwave beeped and Gloria set the potatoes, along with a container of sour cream and a stick of butter, on the table. She grabbed a packet of leftover dinner rolls from the pantry and placed them on the table. "I forgot the green beans."

Paul waved a hand and then pulled out her chair. "Don't worry about it."

They settled in next to each other and bowed their heads. "Dear Lord. Thank you for this food. Thank you for the beautiful day and the beautiful wife you've blessed me with," Paul prayed. "Lord, we pray for Brian, that you recover his memory, you reveal the person who attacked him and also help Gloria decide what to do about Annabelle. Thank you for your Son, our Savior. In Jesus name, we pray. Amen."

"Amen!" Gloria lifted her head and reached for a potato. "Before I forget, I was wondering if it would be okay if Ryan and Tyler spent the night soon. Jill stopped by earlier for a visit. Mally and I had walked back to the creek and we missed them."

Paul placed two slices of meatloaf on his plate and then passed the plate to Gloria. "Of course. I know you would enjoy seeing them. When were you thinking?"

"This weekend," Gloria said. "One more thing. Ben and Kelly invited us to visit them in Houston this summer."

Using the tines of his fork, Paul flattened his potato and then placed a pat of butter on top. "Sure. I've visited Dallas, but never the Houston area. I hear it's a nice area."

Gloria had been there a couple times, but it had been several years. Perhaps flying wouldn't be so bad if Paul went with her. "I'll let them know it's a tentative 'yes' then."

She switched the conversation to Brian's amnesia and mentioned the convicted criminal who had recently escaped and how she had discovered Brian had been involved in his case.

Paul chewed thoughtfully as he listened to her talk. "Interesting. You may be onto something. I wonder if investigators are aware of that."

The fact Brian had lived and there was no murder investigation put the robbery / assault investigation at the bottom of police's priority list. In other words, they probably hadn't done much digging around.

Next, Gloria told him how Brian had placed a help wanted ad in the Green Springs Gazette.

"Now that might be something, too." Paul grabbed the shaker of salt. "Those would definitely be persons of interest."

She also mentioned Rose had a special herbal memory potion she was determined to have Brian try and then she told him Alice had one, as well.

"So all of us, except for Ruth and Margaret, are going to the hospital later to see if we can somehow convince Brian to try them."

Paul scratched his head. "I'm not sure how this is going to work out. Think about it. What person in their right mind would let someone - a complete stranger - give them a potion they claim will restore their memory?"

Gloria shrugged. "It's all we've got. Andrea is desperate. The doctor said it could be a long time before Brian's memory is fully recovered, if ever."

"I can't wait to see how this turns out." Paul reached for another slice of meatloaf and bottle of catsup.

After they finished eating, Gloria and Paul rinsed their dirty dishes and placed them in the dishwasher. She had just enough time to freshen up before driving to Dot's Restaurant to pick up Dot and Rose.

Dot and Rose were standing on the sidewalk, waiting for Gloria when she pulled the SUV into an empty spot. Dot climbed into the passenger side and Rose slid into the back seat.

Gloria glanced in the rearview mirror at Rose. "So what's the plan?"

Chapter 15

Andrea and Alice strolled through the sliding glass doors of Green Springs Memorial Hospital's main entrance.

"Do you have it?" Andrea asked in a low voice.

Alice patted her purse. "Yes. It's in my purse." The women picked up the pace as they strode to the west wing of the hospital where Brian's room was located.

Andrea stopped by the family room first, but Brian's parents weren't in there. "They must be with Brian." Andrea had called to tell them they were on the way.

When the two women stepped into the hospital room, Andrea spotted Brian's parents seated next to the bed. There was also another woman with jet-black hair, hovering off to one side. She turned her gaze when she spotted

Andrea and Alice. Her eyes were the same piercing blue as Brian's eyes.

Joan stood. "Hello Andrea."

Brian turned his attention to Andrea, a small smile on his face. His eyes slid to Alice and the smile disappeared, a thoughtful expression in its place.

"This is Brian's Aunt Beverly."

Andrea stepped to the side and grasped the woman's hand in a firm grip.

"I've heard so much about you," the woman said as she studied Andrea closely.

"Good I hope," Andrea quipped. She turned to Alice. "This is my friend, Alice."

Alice eyed the woman and extended her hand. "Nice to meet you." Judging by the look on Alice's face, Andrea wasn't convinced Alice was being sincere.

Peter Sellers abruptly stood. "The doctor told Brian he's going to release him first thing in the morning."

"Not soon enough," Brian groaned. "This is ridiculous. I feel fine, except for the knot on my noggin."

Joan shifted her gaze and stared at her son. "Better safe than sorry." She leaned down, kissed the side of his cheek and stood. "Now don't you go giving Andrea here a hard time."

"I'll be on my best behavior," her son promised.

Andrea waited until Brian's parents and aunt left the room before focusing her attention on the man in the bed. "I brought Alice by, hoping she might jog your memory."

"When I saw her, I almost remembered. Like I know I've seen you before." His eyes followed Alice as she walked around the side of the bed and stood next to the window. "You love me. In fact, you say to me, 'Alice, if I not marry Andrea,

I marry you. You are the best cook in the whole world!'"

She reached inside her purse and pulled out a round, plastic container. "Your favorite dish is my spicy Mexican soup so I bring you a batch. It's still warm. The hospital food, it not good." Alice reached inside her bag again and pulled out a wrapped set of plastic silverware. "In fact, I bring you silverware to make sure you eat it. It will help your memory, too."

Brian took the container Alice held out, lifted it to eye level and studied the contents. "It looks delicious." He set it on the tray next to his bed.

"You no eat?" Alice leaned forward.

"I just ate." Brian patted his stomach. "A piece of chicken, some rice and a salad. And something akin to Jell-O, although I'm not one hundred percent positive. I'm sure it's not nearly as good as your soup, though."

Alice frowned. "You must eat my soup," she insisted.

"I will," Brian promised. "Later."

Alice tried to wheedle, to cajole, to threaten Brian, all of which seemed to amuse him instead of making him angry, but it was a no-go.

"I need to use the restroom." Alice stomped out of the hospital room and out of sight.

Andrea waited until the sound of her shoes clicking on the hospital corridor faded. "Alice adores you. She'll feel slighted if you don't try her soup."

Brian shifted in the bed. "I will. I promise." He switched the conversation. "I appreciate you spending your time with me and I can see what attracted me to you. You're caring, smart...gorgeous."

Andrea blushed.

"But I feel like a fraud, like I should remember you and I just can't." He pounded his fist on the top of the bedsheet. "It's driving me crazy."

They talked for a few more minutes before Andrea told Brian she had better track down Alice.

Andrea searched the halls, the nearby restroom and the family room. She finally found her pacing back and forth on a small outdoor terrace. "There you are."

Alice stopped pacing. "I wish I could force feed him."

Andrea grinned. "He's stubborn, just like someone else I know."

"When is Rose showing up?" Alice gazed anxiously over the edge of the railing and into the parking lot below.

Andrea glanced at her watch. "Soon. They should be here anytime." It dawned on her that Alice didn't want to give Rose's potion a chance to work. At this point, Andrea was getting desperate. She hoped that at least one of them would work, although there had been a flicker of something in Brian's eyes when he saw Alice.

Why was it he was starting to remember Alice but not her? Maybe he didn't love her as much as she thought. Or worse yet, maybe he did know her and was using this as an excuse to end the relationship!

Tears burned the back of Andrea's eyes.

Alice wrapped her arms around Andrea. "Don't cry cariño. We get him to remember. No worries."

The women talked a few more minutes. Alice would not spend the night and would hitch a ride home with Gloria later. Andrea hoped she and Rose would patch things up. Belhaven was too small of a town to have enemies.

"We better get back inside." Andrea held the door and Alice stepped into the waiting room.

"There you are!" Gloria hurried over. Dot was behind her and Rose brought up the rear. "We couldn't find you earlier. I stopped by Brian's room while Rose and Dot waited here in case you came back. He told me you were around here somewhere."

Andrea explained what had happened and how there had been a flicker of recognition when he saw Alice. She also told them how he hadn't tried Alice's special soup and that it was sitting on the tray next to his bed.

"So it's time for me to put my plan into action?" Rose asked eagerly as she patted the large bulky purse that she was carrying.

Gloria still wasn't certain what Rose's "plan" was. "What exactly is the plan?' she asked.

"You'll see." Rose held up a finger and glanced around the room. "I'll be right back!" She darted across the room and into the restroom, closing the door behind her.

Gloria shifted her gaze to Dot. "Do you know what Rose has up her sleeve?"

"Nope." Dot shook her head. "I can hardly wait to find out."

Gloria, Dot, Andrea, Alice and Lucy chatted about Brian's condition while they waited. Finally, Rose emerged from the bathroom, a wide grin on her face.

Gloria gasped. "What in the world?"

Chapter 16

"Well, what do you think?" Rose twirled in a slow circle as she modeled her medical uniform.

"I dunno," Lucy wrinkled her nose. "Isn't it illegal to impersonate medical staff?"

"It's clever, I'll give you that," Andrea shook her head. "But Lucy may be right. Has Brian met you yet?"

"Nope," Rose shook her head. "Gloria was the only one who visited his room."

Rose shoved her sweater in the bag she was holding before handing the bag to Dot. "Someone needs to track down a tray, maybe a food tray with juice or something so I can take it to Brian along with my special potion."

Alice opened her mouth to protest and quickly closed it. Gloria could tell from the look on her face she hoped Rose got busted.

"You look very professional," Alice muttered and rolled her eyes.

"I saw a tray in the hall." Dot strode across the room and stepped into the hall. She returned moments later with a food tray, a can of soda and an apple. "This is the best I could do on short notice. I snatched it from a tray in the hall."

Rose reached for the tray and placed a small plastic container next to it. "Here goes nothing." Dot held the door while Rose, wearing light blue scrubs, stepped into the hall. She led the way and the others followed at a distance.

Gloria was convinced that at any moment a bona fide medical staff would stop Rose and ask for her ID. She briefly wondered if Rose had created a fake ID. Surely, she wouldn't have gone to that extreme.

The girls hovered in the hall outside Brian's room. Gloria stood closest to the door and tried to eavesdrop on what Rose was saying to Brian.

A nurse – a real nurse – approached the door and started to enter the room.

Andrea lifted her arm, blocking the door. "Wait!"

The nurse abruptly paused. "What?"

"I-uh," Gloria stuttered.

"Mr. Sellers asked us to step outside. He needed to use the bathroom," Lucy blurted out.

"Oh." The nurse took a step back. "I'll come back." She eyed the girls suspiciously before retracing her steps and making her way down the hall. She looked back once and Gloria waved.

"Whew! That was close," Dot groaned. She leaned into the room. "She better hurry up!"

Rose strolled out of Brian's room seconds later, the empty tray under her arm and a triumphant smile on her face. "Mission accomplished!"

"You get him to take your hocus pocus?" Alice pushed past Rose and marched into Brian's room. Andrea was hot on her heels and Gloria not far behind her.

Brian was out of bed, staring out the window. He spun around when Andrea cleared her throat.

Gloria gazed at the table next to the bed and a can of opened soda, a straw sticking out of the top.

Next to the open soda was Alice's soup. The lid was off and a spoon rested inside. "You try my soup?" Alice asked.

"Yes." Brian nodded. "It was delicious. A little on the spicy side but delicious."

Alice shuffled to the hospital over-bed tray and peered into the container. "You eat just enough, but save the rest for later." She winked at Gloria and gave a thumbs up.

She went on. "Andrea is wearing one of your favorite colors. You remember?"

Brian turned on his heel and gazed at Andrea. "No. I mean." He rubbed his temple. The nurse who had attempted to get into Brian's room earlier entered the room and approached the end of the bed. "I have some papers for you to sign, Mr. Sellers, for your release tomorrow. I'll leave them over here." She placed a stack of papers on the tray, next to the can of soda.

"What is this?" The nurse reached for Alice's container of soup and Alice snatched it from her grasp. "It is a special soup Mr. Brian loves."

The nurse shook her head. "You're not allowed to bring food to a patient unless you clear it with the nurse's station."

"You're not supposed to imitate medical staff and sneak into someone's room, either," Alice muttered under her breath.

The nurse leaned forward. "What did you say?"

"Nothing." Alice checked the lid to make sure it was on and then slipped the soup in her purse. She made her way around the bed, grasped Brian's hand and looked into his eyes. "You will be back to normal before you know it. I promise."

Brian placed his hand over the top of Alice's and smiled. "Thank you...Al. I hope so."

Andrea lingered in Brian's room while Dot, Alice, Lucy and Gloria headed to the family waiting room to wait for her. Rose, who had gone ahead, had already changed into her street clothes and was sitting in one of the waiting room chairs when they returned.

Rose popped out of the chair. "Brian drank the whole thing. His memory should be coming back any time now...within hours."

"Yes." Alice clasped her purse in front of her. "He will because he finally eat my special soup."

"And swallowed my special potion," Rose nodded.

"Soup!" Alice insisted.

"Potion!" Rose shot back.

Gloria stepped between them. "Ladies." She stressed the word *ladies*. "Brian appears to have survived your experiments." She glanced at Rose. "At least he's not clucking like a chicken or dancing around the bed post...yet."

Alice snickered.

Gloria turned to her. "And his eyebrows haven't singed off."

Rose snickered back.

"Listen," Gloria continued. "I appreciate both of your efforts and I hope they work, for both Andrea and Brian's sake."

She went on. "As soon as Andrea returns, we'll say our good byes and leave them in peace. We'll have to wait until tomorrow to find out if either – or both – of your self-proclaimed miracle memory potions work."

Andrea wandered into the room a short time later. "Whew! We almost got busted!" She patted Rose's back. "Thanks for putting your neck out there to help me," she said sincerely before turning to Alice. "And you! I think Brian is starting to remember a little. He almost said your name."

She hugged her former housekeeper and Alice lifted a triumphant brow as she gazed at Rose.

Gloria hugged Andrea next. "Good luck dear. We will assume Brian is going home in the morning unless you call and tell us otherwise." She looked at Dot. "I have some new information I discovered earlier to today. We might be onto something." She glanced at her watch. "Paul and I are spending some time together tomorrow, but I think I can sneak away for a quick breakfast if anyone wants to meet me at Dot's Restaurant."

The others agreed to meet Gloria at the restaurant around nine-thirty, after the breakfast crowd cleared and then they left Andrea behind as they headed to the SUV.

Gloria told Rose to hop in the passenger seat while Lucy, Dot and Alice climbed in the rear.

During the drive to Belhaven, she was careful to steer the conversation away from the memory enhancing concoctions and onto the weather, gardening and the recent shut ins.

Eleanor Whittaker, one of the local residents who had been helpful in solving a recent murder mystery, had taken a fall while sweeping off her front steps and had broken her arm.

Gloria was thankful it hadn't been worse, but Eleanor was still having a hard time cooking and baking. Gloria had made an extra effort to stop by at least once a week to visit or to offer to take Eleanor around town to run errands.

Ever since the fall, Eleanor had seemed even frailer and the girls were concerned. She also seemed down in the dumps. Gloria glanced in the rearview mirror. "Do you mind if I give Eleanor a call and ask her to join us in the morning?"

"Oh yes! What a great idea, Gloria," Dot said. "Poor Eleanor."

"Who is Eleanor?" Rose asked. The girls filled her in.

"You can come, too, Alice," Gloria said.

"Oh Miss Gloria! I would love to come, but I promise Mario...Mr. Acosta, I will work at the kennel tomorrow since I not go to work today."

"I understand," Gloria said. "I'm sure Andrea will keep you in the loop on Brian's status."

When they reached town, Gloria dropped Dot and Rose off in front of the restaurant and told them she would see them the next morning.

She dropped Alice off next, and waited until Alice was safely inside the house before backing out of the driveway and turning onto the street.

Lucy was the only one left. "What do you think about Alice and Rose?" she asked.

Gloria tapped her fingernail on the steering wheel. She was certain Rose wasn't trying to step on anyone's toes, including Alice's. If anything, Gloria blamed herself for the current situation.

She should have thought to include Alice, knowing how fond Alice was of Brian and, of course, Andrea.

It was all a misunderstanding and one Gloria hoped to smooth over soon. Occasionally, one of the girls would hurt another's feelings or someone would feel slighted or left out.

Gloria was as guilty as the next person was, especially when she was knee deep in an investigation. Her attention was so focused on the case; she simply forgot to make sure the others were included, unless of course the skill of a certain friend was needed.

She'd asked for Ruth's help with spy equipment, drones, surveillance and snooping numerous times.

Lucy was her go-to girl for weapons.

Margaret was the etiquette queen and business-savvy one of the bunch.

Dot was the levelheaded, sensible one who tried to keep them out of trouble.

Andrea? Well, Andrea was the ambitious one, always wanting to jump right in and get the bad guys. She was all action.

Gloria remembered the time at Mitzi Verona's party where Andrea chased after a suspect, gun strapped to her thigh and then shot the back of the suspect's car.

Yep, Andrea was the wild card...

And Gloria? Well, she was the one who seemed to be right in the thick of things, either by accident or by being asked. She had a nose for trouble and she found *it*...or it found her.

"I think things will settle down. Alice's feathers just got ruffled but it will be okay. Now that we know how she feels, we'll make sure to include her."

Gloria swung into Lucy's driveway and stopped near the house. Lucy scrambled across the back seat and reached for the door handle. "What are you going to do about Annabelle?"

"I don't know," Gloria admitted. "Honestly, I haven't had a lot of time to think about it."

"Annabelle is one of us." Lucy hopped out of the SUV and paused before shutting the door. "I'll see you in the morning." She hurried up the sidewalk to the front of her house.

Gloria gave a quick tap of the horn and waved good-bye before backing out of the drive and heading home. It had been a long day.

Chapter 17

The next morning, Paul puttered in his garage workshop while Gloria headed to town for her breakfast meeting with the girls.

She had spent the night tossing and turning, her thoughts bouncing from one thing to another. She worried about Brian and Andrea, and Alice. She worried about Annabelle and knew Gus was waiting for her to make a decision.

She had forgotten to call her daughter, Jill, to invite her grandsons to spend the night. She was anxious to find out if Andrea would be able to get her hands on Brian's little black schedule book.

Last, but not least, she had forgotten to call Eleanor Whittaker to invite her to breakfast, which was the first thing she did when she crawled out of bed the next morning.

Gloria's heart sank when she heard Eleanor's weak, feeble voice on the other end of the line.

Eleanor perked up when Gloria invited her to join them to discuss the investigation, which made her feel a little better.

Feeling guilty for leaving Paul when she promised they would spend the day together, she cooked a lumberjack breakfast, complete with pancakes, eggs, sausage and toast. She nibbled on a small breakfast plate, saving room for another breakfast at Dot's Restaurant.

Paul called the Montbay County Sheriff's Department first thing, while Gloria was cooking. He told her police were also looking into Walter Tompkins' escape and believed he had not left the state. They had stepped up their search for Tompkins after discovering he had robbed a convenience store in Lansing the night before.

"Lansing," Gloria said as she eyed Paul over the rim of her coffee cup. "That's only about an hour away from here."

Paul poured a generous helping of syrup over the top of his pancakes and cut a chunk off.

"Yeah. It's almost as if he's hanging around, hoping to get picked up."

After breakfast, Gloria told Paul he was off the hook and she would clean up and let Mally out for a run before she headed to Dot's place. She also told him that after tossing and turning half the night, she had decided she wasn't ready to put Annabelle out to pasture and she was going to tell Gus to go ahead and order the replacement parts.

The more Gloria thought about it, the more relieved she was to have made a decision. When she reached the repair shop, she eased into a parking spot and slid out of the SUV before making her way to the front door. Gus was behind the small counter, talking on the phone.

Gloria waited near the window until the conversation ended. "I've made a decision," she announced as he hung up the phone.

"You're gonna repair Annabelle and plan to put at least another hundred thousand miles on her," Gus guessed.

"How did you know?" Gloria propped her purse on the counter and gazed at Gus.

"I know you Gloria. Annabelle is one of the girls. It would be like betraying one of your friends." Gus wiped his forehead with a rag and shoved it in his front pocket. "Hard to find friends like that these days. You're blessed."

A lump formed in Gloria's throat making it hard to speak. There were no truer words spoken. It was hard to find good, got-your-back, solid-in-the-face-of-a-storm friends like hers. She truly was blessed. "Thanks," she managed to croak.

Gus nodded and smiled, the corners of his eyes crinkling. He pulled a clipboard from the drawer, along with a pen and slid them across the counter. "Sign on the dotted line and I'll get the parts ordered today."

Gloria signed and then had Gus add new tires, shocks and brakes to the tally. By the time Gus was done, Annabelle would be like new. She thanked Gus again for the loaner vehicle and headed back out.

She swung by Eleanor's place first. Eleanor must have been waiting for her because Gloria had barely shifted the SUV into park when the front door opened and Eleanor, along with her walker, stepped out onto the stoop.

Gloria hurried to the front door and helped Eleanor down the steps. "You look like a breath of fresh spring air," she told Eleanor as they shuffled to the passenger side of the vehicle.

Eleanor was sporting a short sleeve blouse with an array of brightly colored flowers. She wore a pair of baby blue polyester slacks and bright white tennis shoes. A pair of daisy clip-on earrings completed the ensemble.

"You think so?" Eleanor smoothed her blouse. "I changed three times."

"You look perfect," Gloria said as she opened the passenger door, folded Eleanor's walker and slid it into the back seat of the SUV.

"What happened to Annabelle?"

"She's in Gus's shop getting an overhaul," Gloria explained. She closed Eleanor's door and made her way around the front, climbing behind the wheel.

The women chatted about the weather, Eleanor's broken arm and the robbery at the hardware store on the way to the restaurant. She let Eleanor do most of the talking and the older woman yakked away.

When Gloria pulled into a parking spot in front of the restaurant, she could see Andrea, Margaret, Lucy, Dot and Rose already at the large, round table in the center of the restaurant.

Gloria followed Eleanor into the restaurant and waited until she eased into an empty seat before sliding into the one next to her. She placed her purse on the floor next to her chair. "Where's Ruth?"

"On her way," Lucy said. "She's training a new part-time staffer and was waiting for Kenny to return from his first route delivery."

A tower of donuts sat in the center on the table and coffee cups sat in front of each of the girls, all except for Lucy, who was sipping a tall mocha-colored glass of something.

Gloria pointed at Lucy's drink. "What is that?"

"Iced coffee. Dot just added it to the menu." Lucy slid it toward Gloria. "Here. Try it."

Gloria sipped out of the side of the glass. The cool, chocolatey-coffee flavored concoction was delicious. "Tasty. What do you call it?"

"An iced mocha. Cocoa, sugar, milk, whipped cream, coffee and lots of ice," Dot rattled off the ingredients. "Lucy is my guinea pig. It's something new we're trying."

"Lucy will be your best customer. As long as it has sugar, she'll buy it," Margaret joked.

"So we've managed to perfect it?" Rose asked.

"Almost," Lucy said. "It could use a pinch more sugar, but that's my personal preference."

"Which means it's perfect the way it is," Andrea teased.

Ruth wandered in a few minutes later and slid into the last empty seat. "Whew! I hope Brian's memory returns soon and he re-opens the hardware store. I've never heard so many people grumble and gripe because it's closed."

"Never mind how Brian almost lost his life," Gloria said as she shook her head. "Speaking of that, is Brian being released from the hospital today?"

Andrea averted her gaze, shifting her focus on the donut and the plate in front of her. "Yes. His parents are there now. He should be home by noon."

She went on. "So far, he hasn't remembered anything else." She gave Rose a quick glance. "We're hoping once he gets home, familiar surroundings will jog his memory."

Andrea's lower lip began to tremble and she sucked in a breath. "Before I left, he asked me to give him some space. He said he's confused and needs to spend time alone."

A small tear trickled down Andrea's cheek. "If his memory doesn't return soon, I'm going to officially call off the wedding."

Chapter 18

"Call off the wedding?" Gloria blinked rapidly. "I..." She turned to Lucy, a look of helplessness on her face.

"Are you sure you want to do that Andrea? I mean, you've already ordered the dress, picked out the flowers, settled on a caterer and musicians," Lucy argued. "You'll lose deposit money on the photographer."

The tears freely streamed down Andrea's cheeks and Gloria's heart broke for her young friend. She reached out and squeezed her hand. Not long ago, she had been in a similar situation where Paul had to leave town unexpectedly days before their wedding and Gloria had become despondent.

"Oh dear," Eleanor reached for her water glass, her eyes watering, too. "Such a shame."

"We're going to get to the bottom of this," Gloria vowed. "Andrea. Give us a chance to dig into this case. Don't do anything for..." her voice trailed off as she gazed at her friends sitting around the table.

"A week," Dot said. "Give Gloria a week."

"Okay. I guess it won't matter," Andrea's shoulders sagged. "I've decided to take a break myself. I'm going to visit my parents in Nantucket. They vacation there every year." Andrea swiped at her tear stained cheeks with the back of her hand. "I'm leaving in the morning."

"What a wonderful idea. Some sea breezes and sunshine will do you good." Gloria said. "Why don't we pray?"

The women joined hands and bowed their heads. "Dear Heavenly Father. We pray this morning for our dear friend, Andrea. Lord, you know the situation, you know Andrea's heartbreak over Brian and how she's thinking of calling off the wedding. Please guide us Father. Give us the wisdom and the tools to find the person or persons who attacked Brian and robbed him of his memory. We also ask you return Brian's full memory...soon. Thank you for your Son, our Savior, Jesus Christ."

"Amen" echoed around the room.

Andrea attempted a half-hearted smile. "I feel better already."

Lucy pushed her chocolate covered donut across the table to Andrea. "Here. You can have my donut. Chocolate always helps, at least for me it does."

The conversation shifted to the investigation. Gloria told the girls what she had discovered, how Walter Tompkins had recently escaped from prison and that Brian had reviewed his case.

She also told the others how Brian had placed a help-wanted ad in the Green Springs Gazette and Andrea had said he had started interviewing potential employees.

Dot nibbled the end of her glazed donut. "Is there any way we can find out if anyone had been scheduled to come in for an interview the morning of the robbery?"

"Yes." Andrea nodded. "Brian keeps a black appointment book at home but now that he doesn't want me around..." Her face crumpled and tears threatened a second time.

Lucy patted her shoulder. "Stay strong, Andrea. We'll help you through this," she encouraged.

Andrea sucked in a breath. "With the way his mind is working right now, I'm not sure he has even thought about trying to figure out who did this to him."

"We could break into his house," Ruth suggested.

All eyes turned to Ruth.

"What? It's not like we haven't done that before," she pointed out.

Rose, who had been sipping on her coffee, began to gag. "You break into people's houses?" she choked.

"Only when absolutely necessary," Margaret assured her.

"Which has been just about every single time," Dot groaned.

"Lord have mercy!" Rose slammed her open palm on the table. "Have you ever been caught...arrested?"

"Yeah," Gloria sighed. "Both, unfortunately. It's a hazard of the job, I'm afraid. My first arrest was a murder charge, not breaking and entering."

"Oh my goodness gracious," Rose gasped. "Good thing you're married to a police officer."

"Retired," Gloria corrected. "I've never tested it, but he would probably leave me in jail if I got arrested for breaking and entering."

"Nah!" Ruth waved her hand. "Paul would post bail."

"Eventually." Gloria changed the subject. "If we don't break in, I could go visit under the guise of checking on him to make sure he doesn't need anything," she offered.

"Nope." Andrea shook his head. "He said he wanted to be alone, as in everyone leave him alone. He even named you specifically...Ginger."

Ruth snorted. "He thinks Gloria's name is Ginger?"

Andrea nodded. "Yeah. I have a key but he's probably on his way home and I'm leaving in the morning."

"There has to be a way to get inside his house and track down the black book without him finding out what we're up to," Gloria swiped an imaginary crumb off the table.

Ruth leaned back in her chair and crossed her arms. "I have an idea, but I need to mull it over, work out the details first."

Gloria watched as Sally Keane, the Quik Stop corner grocery store employee, passed by the large front picture window. She held up a hand. "Wait! Has anyone thought to talk to Brian's employees to see if perhaps Brian mentioned something to them?"

Andrea stared at Gloria blankly. "Why didn't I think of that?"

All eyes turned to Ruth. "You're not going to clue us in on your idea?" Lucy asked as she reached for her iced mocha.

Ruth gazed around the table at the eager faces. "Like I said, I have a couple details to work out first. It's still in the planning stages."

Whatever it was, Gloria was onboard. Ruth was an expert in her field of spy and surveillance so she was certain whatever it was involved her arsenal of equipment. She glanced at her watch and jumped out of her chair. "I better get going. Paul and I are having a date day and I don't want to be late."

"I'll give Eleanor a ride home," Margaret offered.

Gloria had completely forgotten about poor Eleanor. "Thanks Margaret. That would be great." She reached for her purse, still next to her chair. "I'll make my rounds tomorrow morning to talk to Brian's employees," she promised before heading out the door.

Chapter 19

Paul and Gloria spent the afternoon in Green Springs watching a matinee movie, munching on popcorn and enjoying a little down time. The movie, a mystery thriller, was one Gloria had been anxiously waiting to come out for months. Parts of the movie reminded her of the classic, *Murder on the Orient Express*.

After the movie, they wandered in and out of the quaint shops in the heart of Green Springs, the apothecary, a dime store that still sported the creaky old wooden floors and a gift shop. Their last stop was a thrift store where Gloria found a vintage orange metal coffee mug tree straight out of the 70's that would fit perfectly in the corner of her kitchen counter.

When they finished window-shopping, they wandered back to the loaner vehicle. Paul held the door while Gloria climbed into the SUV and reached for her seatbelt.

She watched as he made his way around the front of the vehicle and slid behind the wheel. "Where did you say you were taking me for dinner?"

Paul buckled his seatbelt and smiled at his wife. "I didn't. It's a surprise." He eased the SUV onto the road and they drove to the next town, Rapid Creek, and to Lake Harmony.

"Are we going to do the dinner boat cruise again?" Paul had surprised her with a romantic dinner boat cruise last year. It had been a wonderful evening.

He shook his head. "No. Close, though."

He turned onto a small paved drive and a narrow, winding path. They rounded the corner and straight ahead was a large, Victorian manor. "This...this is the Garfield place," Gloria guessed.

The Garfield place was a well-known, historic home in Montbay County. It had a colorful history...some would say deep and dark, with whispers of mafia ties, money laundering and murder.

Gloria had never been inside the stately home. Several years ago, rumor had it the place had fallen into disrepair and the owners were considering bulldozing it.

The Rapid Creek historical society had stepped in, vowing to save the manor. They spent several months raising money to restore the grand home to its original splendor.

After the restoration, the city, hard up for cash, had put it up for sale and an unknown party had purchased it. It was the last Gloria had heard of the home...until now.

"I did a little research to find the perfect place for a special dinner and found this was now not only a bed and breakfast, but they also serve dinner." Paul pulled into a parking spot, shifted into park and turned the SUV's engine off.

"So far it's getting rave reviews." He climbed out of the car, walked around the front and over to the passenger side. Paul opened the door and held out his hand. "I figured you would love the mystery and intrigue of the place."

"Oh yes!" Gloria squeezed Paul's hand. "This is perfect," she gushed. They wandered down the cobblestone sidewalk and onto the spacious front porch.

The home, a stormy blue gray color with stark white trim and corner turrets, looked haunted. A corner bay window graced the front and an expansive porch welcomed guests. Porch lights blazed brightly.

Gloria gazed at one of the small windows in the peak of the roof and the hair on the back of her neck stood up. "That must be the attic," she mumbled under her breath.

They made their way through the front entrance and over to the hostess station. "Kennedy, party of two," Paul told the woman.

She studied the open guest book in front of her and then nodded. "Follow me."

Gloria's heels clicked on the gleaming mahogany floor as she followed the woman, all the while studying the sparkling chandeliers and elegant tables for two and four. "I think I'm under-dressed," she whispered to her husband as she gazed at the other diners.

"You look fine," Paul reassured her as he placed his hand on the small of her back.

The hostess stopped in front of a table for two near a tall window. At the top of the window were panes of stained glass. The window overlooked an expansive garden.

Paul waited for Gloria to sit and pushed her chair in before settling into the seat across from her. The hostess handed them each a menu. "Your server will be right with you."

"The dinners must cost a fortune," Gloria said as she reached for her reading glasses.

"You're worth every penny."

Gloria slipped her glasses on and studied the menu. The selection was limited but varied, with offerings of fish, steak and seafood.

The server arrived with two glasses of ice water, easing them next to the wrapped silverware. "I recommend trying the three-course dinner," she said.

Gloria decided on a wedge salad with blue cheese crumbles and buttermilk dressing to start. For an entrée, she chose pan-fried perch while Paul chose the house salad and rack of lamb.

The server jotted down their orders and told them she would return shortly with their salads. "A toast." Paul lifted his glass of water. "To the most beautiful woman in the room."

Gloria lifted her glass and tapped his lightly. "To the best husband a woman could ever ask for." She sipped her water and set the glass next to her plate.

"How is Andrea doing?" They hadn't yet discussed Brian's current situation. Paul listened quietly as Gloria told him Brian needed some "space," and wanted to be left alone.

She also told him Andrea was threatening to call off the wedding but promised Gloria and the girls she would postpone her decision for a few days. In the meantime, she was heading to Nantucket to spend time with her parents and take a much-needed break from the tragic situation.

Gloria was certain her young friend had gotten little sleep after spending the last couple of nights at the hospital. Perhaps it was best if Brian and Andrea spend a few days apart.

She started to tell him how Rose posed as a nurse to get Brian to take her special potion, but stopped short, convinced he would not be pleased that Rose had impersonated a nurse.

Instead, she told him she intended to chat with Brian's other employees the following day.

Their salads arrived and the conversation paused. Gloria shifted her plate and studied the wedge of lettuce. "I should eat more salads," she said.

Paul unfolded his napkin and placed it on his lap. "It probably wouldn't hurt either of us."

Gloria sliced a wedge of lettuce and dipped it in the dressing. "How did Allie's interview at the Montbay County Sheriff's Department go?"

Paul told her Allie had gotten the job and would be starting the following Monday. He could see the wheels turning in his wife's head. "Don't get any bright ideas of dragging Allie into your investigations," he warned Gloria.

"Me?" Gloria batted her eyes innocently. "Why I wouldn't..." she trailed off, unable to promise him she wouldn't involve her new stepdaughter. "I'll try," she finished lamely.

Their entrees arrived not long after they finished eating their salads. Gloria sliced a small piece of the perch and chewed thoughtfully. "This is delicious. Try a bite." She sliced off a second piece and held the fork out for Paul to try.

He agreed it was delicious before offering her a bite of his lamb, which Gloria had never tried before.

She nibbled a small piece and thanked him for sharing. It was an acquired taste she decided and declined another taste.

The dinner portions were the perfect size and Gloria must have been hungrier than she thought because she cleaned her plate, leaving not a single morsel of fish or bite of potato wedge behind.

The server cleared their table and returned a short time later with an array of mouth-watering desserts. She lowered the tray so that Paul and Gloria had an unobstructed view. "Vanilla crème brûlée, white chocolate cheesecake, toasted coconut and caramel cake, and molten lava cake with a side of vanilla bean ice cream," the woman rattled off the desserts on display.

The molten lava cake caught Gloria's eye and she quickly chose that dessert while Paul opted for the white chocolate cheesecake. "Coffee?"

"Yes, please," he nodded. "Decaf though."

The server shifted the tray and nodded. "I'll be right back."

Gloria watched the woman leave and then turned to her husband. "The food is delicious. I wonder if they offer tours of the estate. I would love to take a tour of this place."

When the desserts arrived, Gloria posed the question to their server, who told her that on Tuesday afternoons, they hosted a high tea and after tea, the owners offered a guided tour of both the home and grounds.

"I should bring the girls," Gloria decided. "Perhaps when Andrea returns from her trip, we can plan an afternoon here. This might give her some great ideas for her tea room."

Andrea had planned to open a tearoom, but the plan had been put on the backburner after her recent engagement to Brian.

Gloria dug into her dessert, filling her spoon with a small piece of cake and topping it with the chocolate. She closed her eyes, savoring the spoon full of warm, creamy melted chocolate. "This is one of the best desserts ever."

They sipped their coffee and shared their decadent desserts as they discussed the movie they had watched earlier. Finally, it was time to leave. Paul paid the bill and they stepped out onto the porch.

When they reached the sidewalk, Gloria noticed another path leading around the side of the magnificent manor. "I wonder if we can take a look at the lake." She didn't wait for Paul to answer as she started down the path.

The sprawling rear yard was lush and green, and the smell of lilacs filled the air. The lake was smooth as glass. A small boathouse jutted out into the water and the setting sun cast a glimmering path.

A flash of light from one of the boathouse windows caught her eye. "Did you see that?"

"See what?" Paul asked.

"Never mind. I guess my eyes are playing tricks on me." She shrugged and slipped her hand in Paul's hand. They stood silently soaking in the view before turning back.

The hair on the back of Gloria's neck stood up again as they retraced their steps. She glanced back at the boathouse. "Maybe I don't want to do a tour," she shivered.

Gloria was quiet during the ride home, her mind on poor Andrea. What if Brian never remembered her? Was it possible to fall in love with the same person twice?

She gave Paul a sideways glance. God planned a person's steps according to His will. She was convinced Paul and she were meant to be together. Was God somehow intervening in Andrea and Brian's life?

Gloria had been so caught up in what was going on in her world; she had forgotten to ask Paul what his plans were for the following day.

He told her he was going to run by the sheriff's station to see what his former co-workers were up to and if they'd heard of any security detail jobs he might be able to pick up.

Paul was enjoying retirement but Gloria knew there were days he rattled around the farm, not sure what to do with himself. Allie had kept him busy with her move and helping her settle into the farm. He had finished repairing his ice shanty and cleaned the barn.

"That sounds like a good idea." While Paul was struggling to stay busy, Gloria rarely had a chance to catch her breath!

Mally was waiting for them when they pulled into the drive and Gloria could see her snout pressed tight against the windowpane as she watched them exit the SUV and head toward the porch.

Gloria opened the porch door and Mally darted past her, racing straight over to her favorite tree. She came to a screeching halt near the bottom of the tree and began barking her head off.

The squirrels were having great fun teasing poor Mally as they darted from branch to branch, stopping every so often to look down at her, which only set Mally off again.

Finally, Mally gave up, followed her standard patrol around the farm and headed back to the porch. Gloria patted her head. "Darn squirrels. Just once, one of them should scamper down from the tree to say hello."

Paul was already inside when Gloria made her way in. He was standing in the corner of the kitchen, next to the answering machine and house telephone. "You're gonna want to hear this," he said as he pressed the play button.

Chapter 20

"Hey Gloria. Margaret here. I've been trying to call you on your cell phone but it keeps going to voice mail. I thought you might want to know there's an ambulance parked in Brian's driveway. They've been sitting there for a good half hour now."

Margaret lowered her voice. "Call me back when you have a minute." The call ended. Gloria hurried to her purse, pulled her cell phone out and turned it on. Not only had Margaret called, but also Dot, Lucy, Andrea and Ruth.

"Uh-oh. I think something big is going down."

Paul headed to the living room while Gloria dialed Margaret's number first. It went directly to voice mail. She tried each of her friend's phones, right on down the line and each call went straight to voice mail.

Gloria gazed out the window. It was getting dark and she had planned to kick back and have a quiet evening at home with Paul. There was no way she would be able to relax until she found out what was going on at Brian's place.

Worry over her friend won out and she headed to the living room. "Margaret called to say there was an ambulance at Brian's house. She called about a half an hour ago. I must not have heard it ringing in my purse. I tried to call her back but she didn't answer and neither did any of the other girls. They all tried calling."

She went on. "I'm going to run down there to see what's going on."

"I'll go with you." Paul lowered the footrest on his recliner and climbed out of the chair. They hopped back into the SUV and pulled out onto the road.

"It's a good thing Gus isn't charging mileage," Gloria joked.

It was a few minutes back into town. When they reached town and the flashing light, Paul turned right and headed toward the lake.

Paul and Gloria had visited Brian at his spacious, modern home that overlooked the lake several times. It was a beautiful home, and something straight out of the Architectural Digest magazine.

The pavement ended and Paul slowed the vehicle when they reached a sharp turn and gravel part of the road. As soon as they cleared the bend, Gloria could see an ambulance parked in Brian's drive, its lights flashing. Parked next to the ambulance was a Montbay County fire truck.

A crowd had gathered on the edge of the front lawn. The SUV's lights illuminated the cluster of onlookers and Gloria spotted Lucy's red hair. Standing next to Lucy was Andrea, Margaret and the other girls.

Paul eased onto the side of the road, shut off the engine and they climbed out.

Gloria made her way over to Margaret. "What happened?" Margaret spun around. "Gosh! You scared me." She shook her head. "We don't know. I noticed the lights when I headed out onto my back deck. It was hard to see whose house the ambulance had gone to, but something told me it was Brian's house."

Andrea, who was standing next to Margaret, grasped Gloria's hand. "I...I tried to go up there, but remembered Brian told me to stay away. Alice saw the lights on her way home from the dog-training center. She told me about it as soon as she got home so we walked down here to see if we could find out what was going on."

Lucy scratched her forehead. "I wish we knew what was happening."

Gloria turned to her husband. Paul knew most, if not all, of the area police, paramedics and emergency personnel, not to mention firefighters. "Can you go check it out?"

Paul shifted his gaze, nodded to his wife and eased out of the crowd before heading up the sloped drive to the front door. Moments later, he disappeared inside.

Gloria began to pace. "What if he had a relapse?"

"Or someone broke into his house and attacked him," Margaret added.

"Bite your tongue," Ruth said.

A dark figure emerged from the house. It was Paul. He headed back down the hill. The girls crowded around when he got close. "I guess Brian had just gotten home and began to have chest pains. He tried to rest but when it got worse, his mother became alarmed and called an ambulance."

Paul glanced back at the house. "He told them that someone had given him some very spicy food and now paramedics suspect it may be a case of severe indigestion."

Gloria turned to Alice. "Alice?"

"Why...I. My spicy food. It never give me indigestion!" she argued.

"That's because you're used to it," Gloria said. She looked at her husband. "Did they say anything else?"

Paul sucked in a breath. "Brian named an 'Alice' as the person who gave him the spicy food and hinted that perhaps she was trying to take him out."

Alice's eyes widened. She clutched the bottom of her blouse. "I-I try to help. No one ever died from eating my spice." She turned accusing eyes to Rose, who hovered nearby.

Gloria hadn't noticed her standing there before.

"You!" Alice pointed an accusing finger at Rose. "Whatever you gave Brian. It make him ill!"

Rose stiffened her back. "I most certainly did not. My memory cure may smell bad, but it never killed nobody!"

"You don't think," Gloria rubbed her chin thoughtfully. "That the two mixtures – Alice and Rose's concoctions, caused Brian to think he was having a heart attack."

Andrea pressed both hands to her cheeks. "Great! Now, not only does Brian not want me, he thinks I'm trying to kill him!"

A commotion near the front porch stopped Gloria from answering. The paramedics, along with the firefighters emerged. There was one other person in the crowd – Officer Joe Nelson. The paramedics climbed into the ambulance while the firefighters climbed into the fire truck.

The crowd of onlookers shifted to the side and Gloria watched as they pulled out of the drive and onto the road, revealing Officer Joe Nelson's patrol car, which had been hidden by the emergency vehicles. Instead of getting into his cruiser, Officer Nelson made his way down the hill.

He approached the onlookers, his eyes scanning the crowd. He paused when he spied Andrea. "Can I have a word with you?" He motioned her to the other side of the driveway and out of earshot. Alice trailed behind.

Gloria couldn't hear what was being said. Andrea spoke quickly and motioned toward the house a couple times. She put a protective arm around Alice's shoulder and kept shaking her head.

Gloria couldn't stand it. She slipped away from the crowd and strode over to the trio. "What is going on?"

"Brian is accusing Alice of trying to poison him so Officer Nelson asked Alice to accompany him to the sheriff's station to answer a few questions," Andrea whispered in a low voice.

"Can she meet you there?" Gloria asked Officer Nelson. "Think of how this will look with all of the townsfolk watching."

Officer Nelson looked from Gloria to the crowd hovering nearby. "I dunno."

Paul approached and Gloria briefly explained the situation. He nodded slowly. "What if I drive her there myself?" Paul asked.

"It's not like she's under arrest," Gloria pointed out.

Officer Nelson caved and Paul promised they would follow him to the station. "Okay, but only if Paul accompanies you."

Officer Nelson shifted his attention to the onlookers. He began waving his hands. "Party is over folks. Time to go home."

Alice marched over to Rose, who was following Dot to her van. "Not so fast! You're going to the police station, too!"

Chapter 21

Despite Rose's insistence she was innocent and the whole thing had nothing to do with her, Dot convinced her they should follow the others to the sheriff's department to try to help clear Alice's name.

Andrea and Alice slid into the back of the SUV while Paul got behind the wheel and Gloria climbed into the passenger seat.

"This will all be cleared up as soon as we get there." Gloria attempted to convince Alice that everything would turn out all right but her words rang hollow. What if police suspected Alice was behind the hardware store robbery and when Brian survived the attack, she tried to poison him?

Surely, police would realize Alice was harmless. There was no way she could overpower Brian. Unless, of course, she took him by surprise and hit him in the back of the head, which was exactly what had happened. A surprise attack.

"I can vouch for you the morning of the attack," Andrea assured her.

Gloria silently wondered if vouching for Alice would make matters worse and implicate both Alice and Andrea.

Paul did a U-turn and started to follow Officer Nelson's patrol car. Dot and Rose brought up the rear. The vehicles drove out of town as they headed to Langstone, where the Montbay Sheriff's station was located.

Andrea leaned forward in her seat. "We're dragging Rose into this since she gave Brian a special memory mixture too. I'm not sure how wise it would be to tell police that Rose impersonated a nurse to get Brian to take her concoction."

"Impersonated a nurse!" Paul glanced in the rearview mirror. "Rose impersonated medical personnel?" He turned to his bride who shrank back in her seat.

"I-uh. By the time I knew what she was doing, it was too late," Gloria said lamely. "No one was hurt."

"Except Brian," Paul argued. He ran a hand through his hair. "Gloria Kennedy! What if Brian puts two and two together and realizes Rose had been in his room impersonating a nurse?"

Paul had a good point. Rose was a big, buxom dark-skinned woman with a loud, booming voice. In other words, she stood out in a crowd.

"Looking back, it was probably the wrong thing to do," Gloria admitted. She shifted in her seat and gazed at Alice who sat silently stewing in the back seat. "Alice. We might need to keep Rose's involvement on the down low."

"I hope they arrest her," Alice gritted through her teeth. "That woman. It is her fault we're in this predicament! She mix her potion with my spicy soup and Brian had reaction."

Gloria remembered how Rose had said there were side effects to her memory mixture. She decided it was best not to share that information with Paul. He was already freaking out about the nurse thing.

"At least Brian is okay," she repeated a second time and then decided not to add anything else lest she throw herself even further under the bus.

Officer Nelson's vehicle was parked out front and Paul parked next to the patrol car. Dot, who was right behind them, pulled into an empty spot on the other side.

They all filed into the station where Officer Nelson, who stood waiting at the counter, cast a puzzled glance at Dot and Rose. "What…"

Paul shoved his hands in his front pockets. "There's more to the story. I'll let the girls explain."

Officer Nelson frowned. "Why am I not surprised?" He waved his hand. "Follow me."

They made their way down the long hall to one of the rooms near the back. Gloria hadn't been in the station for several months, not since Lucy had been questioned about her ex-boyfriend's murder the previous fall.

Paul stood near the door while Officer Nelson squeezed his way behind the desk and the girls - Dot, Rose, Andrea, Alice and Gloria sat on the other side.

Alice primly placed her purse in her lap. "I did not poison Mr. Brian. She did!" She pointed an accusing finger at Rose who was already shaking her head.

"Oh no. I most certainly did not. No one has ever gotten sick on my memory enhancing elixir. I smelled your mess," Rose shot back. "It would singe the hair off a hippie."

The two women began to bicker back and forth, each of them blaming the other for Brian's symptoms. Finally, Officer Nelson had had enough. "Ladies!"

The women grew silent.

"I'm sorry," Rose apologized first.

"Me too," Alice mumbled.

"I'm gathering from what Brian told me and what you've just said that you both gave Brian some sort of 'miracle cure' for his memory loss." He lowered his chin and gave them both a hard stare. "Neither of which worked, I might add."

Rose lifted a hand and inspected her nails. "Give it time. I hasn't even been a day."

He ignored Rose's comment and continued. "Look, I know everyone is trying to help here, but you can't just go around willy-nilly drugging people."

Alice started to speak but Officer Nelson raised a hand to stop her. "Let me finish. I'm going to talk to Brian and advise him to let the incident slide on one condition…"

Gloria could see it coming now…their warning.

"You must promise to stay away from Mr. Sellers and his home." He shifted his gaze to Andrea. "That includes you."

Andrea's lower lip started to tremble.

Officer Nelson reached a hand across the desk toward Andrea. "Give him a little time. I'm sure he'll come around and remember you. If not, you're a lovely young woman and even if he can't remember, he'll probably fall in love with you all over."

"I-thank you for letting us off with a warning." Andrea, determined not to cry, blinked rapidly. "I'm leaving for Massachusetts in the morning so that won't be a problem."

The others, taking the cue and not wanting to push their luck, stood. "Thank you, Officer Nelson. We'll be on our best behavior," Gloria promised and turned to the others. "Right?"

"Right," the girls echoed, nodding solemnly.

Paul opened the door and held it while the girls filed out of the room.

Officer Nelson was the last one out. He turned to Paul. "You think my warning will work?"

Paul rolled his eyes. "I give it a 50/50 chance. Knowing my wife..." He shook his head.

Officer Nelson slapped Paul on the back. "You sign on for that security detail starting tomorrow?"

Paul had been able to land a week's temporary assignment covering a growing statewide disarmament group, who was holding a convention in downtown Grand Rapids, which by itself wasn't a big of a concern. It was the fact that the convention center had also booked a regional rifle association convention for the same dates.

Police and officials were anticipating a few clashes and had hired extra security to cover the event.

"Yep, I'll be there." Paul eyed the back of his wife's head. "Maybe I should reconsider given my wife's penchant for mischief."

"Whew! You sure have your hands full." Officer Nelson walked them to the front door and with one last word of warning, told them they were free to leave.

The girls exited the building and gathered near the back of the SUV. "Well, that went over well," Dot said.

"Right?" Andrea shifted her purse on her shoulder. She told the others she had tried to tell Brian about the black planner book but by then, Brian was already hinting he wanted some "space" so she hadn't gotten around to it. "At this point, I'm ready for a break myself and a few extra days isn't going to hurt anything."

Gloria nodded her agreement, but in the back of her mind, she knew that with every day that went by, the case grew colder and the chances of figuring out who attacked Brian, more difficult.

There was no harm in Gloria stopping by to chat with Brian's employees, starting with Officer Joe Nelson's girlfriend, Sally Keane, who happened to work at the Quik Stop.

Chapter 22

Gloria waited until Paul had left for his temporary job the following morning before settling in for another cup of coffee and quiet time to read her Bible. She slipped her reading glasses on, flipped her Bible open to the marker and read Ephesians 6:12-13 NIV:

"For our struggle is not against flesh and blood, but against the rulers, against the authorities, against the powers of this dark world and against the spiritual forces of evil in the heavenly realms.

Therefore put on the full armor of God, so that when the day of evil comes, you may be able to stand your ground, and after you have done everything, to stand."

Gloria lifted her gaze and stared out the window as she sipped her coffee. She hadn't read the Bible verse in a long time and it struck her how God was speaking to her through his word.

It seemed the world had changed, even more so the past few years, that evil was gaining the upper hand, in the public schools, the workplace and even in the most sacred of sanctuaries...home.

Gloria lowered her head, closed her eyes and prayed a heartfelt prayer for not only her own family and friends, but also the country she loved so much and worried about where it was headed.

Gloria lifted her head and wiped a lone tear that had escaped. God was in control and instead of focusing on all the negative and evil, she would trust in the One who controlled the universe.

After Gloria finished the last of her coffee, she threw on a pair of yard shoes and Mally and she wandered outdoors to inspect the garden.

They passed by Mally's tree. Two robins twittered and chirped as they flitted from branch to branch, as if overseeing the garden's progress for themselves.

The morning air was cool and crisp. By the time Mally and Gloria headed back inside, Gloria's cheeks were rosy and chilled from the morning air. She quickly showered and headed back to the kitchen to grab her things.

Gloria had offered to drive Andrea to the airport so she wouldn't have to pay to park her car but Andrea refused, telling Gloria it would be good for her to spend some time alone.

Alice had finally gotten her driver's license but refused to drive any further than around Belhaven. It was a huge step for Alice and allowed her a small amount of independence.

Gloria took a few moments to check her email and there was a note from Mary Beth, telling her the car parts would arrive the following day and Gus would start working on Annabelle as soon as they arrived.

The more Gloria drove the SUV, the more convinced she was that she had made the right decision to repair Annabelle instead of purchase the SUV, which had zero personality or little quirks that made Annabelle unique.

With a quick check to make sure she'd turned the coffee pot off, Gloria slipped on a light jacket, grabbed the keys from the hook and her purse from the chair.

She hurried to the SUV, unlocked the driver's side door and slid behind the wheel. Her plan was to park at the far end of Main Street, in front of Nails and Knobs. Gloria's first stop would be the local pharmacy.

She easily found a parking spot in front of the dark, empty hardware store. Gloria wondered what would happen to the three stores if Brian's memory never returned.

Perhaps he would sell everything and move back to a place in his life he remembered. Gloria couldn't imagine what that would be like...frustrating to say the very least.

Gloria passed by the small barbershop. Next to the barbershop was Thelma's Thrift Shop, which only opened one or two days a week. On the other side of the thrift store was the pharmacy.

Gloria made her way up the small ramp to the entrance, pushed the door open and stepped inside. The pungent smell of mothballs caused her to wrinkle her nose. It had been several months since Gloria had been inside the pharmacy and there had been some changes.

Off to the right was the front counter and behind the counter, Gladys McTavish. Gladys was somewhat new to Belhaven, having only lived in the area for a decade or so after marrying Stan McTavish, a retired used car salesman from Green Springs.

Rumor had it Gladys and Stan had met via an online dating site, at least that's what Ruth had told Gloria.

Gloria had seen her around town now and then. Although Gladys worked at the pharmacy, she rarely patronized the area businesses including Dot's Restaurant. Once in a blue moon, Gladys' husband, Stan, would have coffee with some of the other retirees down at Dot's Restaurant.

Ruth didn't care for Gladys and Gloria wondered if it was because she just didn't know her that well since the woman kept to herself.

To the left of the entrance were rows of sundries including a rack of magazines, snack foods and suntan lotion. In the back of the store was another counter, this one higher than the front checkout counter. Hidden behind the counter was the pharmacy.

Spring meant bath time for Mally so Gloria grabbed a handbasket and headed for the small pet supply section. She picked up a bottle of pet shampoo and turned it over. "Hm. The prices are pretty reasonable."

She stopped one aisle over, grabbed a box of Band-Aids, some nail polish remover and headed to the front with her purchases.

Gladys was a tall, thin woman, and as Gloria got closer, she noticed a large scar on her chin. She tried not to gawk but the scar was so prominent, it was hard for her eyes not to be drawn to it. She averted her gaze and stared at the items in her basket instead. "Good morning."

"Good morning," Gladys replied pleasantly.

"It's going to be a beautiful day," Gloria said.

"Yes," Gladys said.

The conversation stalled and Gloria racked her brain in an attempt to keep the conversation going. "It's a shame about your boss, Brian Sellers."

"For sure." Gladys reached inside the basket and grabbed the dog shampoo.

No wonder Ruth wasn't a fan of Gladys! The woman hardly talked, unlike Ruth who loved to chat, to gossip...

"He's home now. Hopefully he'll be back to work soon," Gloria lifted the empty basket off the counter and placed it on top of the nearby stack.

"That's good." Gladys watched Gloria set the basket down.

Gloria's eyes were drawn to the scar again, and before she could stop herself, she blurted out. "What a wicked scar." She immediately wished she could take back the words but it was too late!

Gladys self-consciously touched the scar with her index finger. "Yes."

"I'm sorry...I mean I didn't." Gloria fumbled over her words. Not wanting to make an already uncomfortable exchange worse, she clamped her mouth shut and waited for Gladys to scan her debit card. Gladys scanned the card and handed the card, along with a store receipt, to Gloria.

"Thank you. Have a nice day." Gloria grabbed her purchases and headed for the door. She could feel Gladys' eyes following her.

When she reached the sidewalk in front of the drug store, she looked back. "Well, that went well."

On the other side of the drugstore was Kip's Bar and Grill. Next to Kip's was a vacant building and then Dot's Restaurant. She started to head inside Dot's when she changed her mind and continued walking toward the Quik Stop. First things first.

The bell chimed merrily as Gloria pushed the door open and stepped inside. Brian had recently remodeled the interior of the grocery store and added onto the back. A deli counter filled the entire back wall, offering a variety of deli meats and cheeses as well as a mouthwatering selection of artisan breads.

Large selections of gourmet spreads were on display next to the deli and on the other side, a pastry case filled with tempting sweet treats. Brian was giving Dot a run for her money.

Gloria glanced at the checkout counter and Sally Keane, who was behind the counter and rummaging through the cash register. She glanced up when she heard the doorbell. "Oh hi Gloria!"

She slammed the cash register shut and placed both hands on the counter, giving Gloria her full attention. "Sorry if I seem jumpy. Ever since Brian was robbed, I'm a nervous nelly. I keep thinking every person who walks through the door is going to rob me."

Sally was a talker, and a complainer, unlike Gladys McTavish who was a woman of few words.

"Poor Brian." Gloria shook her head. "He can't remember anything that happened."

Sally snorted. "Or that he's engaged to Andrea Malone. Speaking of engaged." Sally's hand shot out and she fluttered her fingers in front of Gloria. "Joe finally proposed."

Gloria took a step closer. "Well I'll be," she said. *Officer Joe Nelson had officially gone off the deep end!* "Congratulations."

Sally lifted her hand to inspect her sparkler. "Yeah. We're going to have a summer wedding. It will be the biggest event in all of Montbay County now that Andrea and Brian's wedding has been called off. Not that I blame him. I mean, who would want to marry a complete stranger?"

The tips of Gloria's ears began to burn as Sally hinted that perhaps Brian was faking his amnesia to get out of the engagement. The palm of Gloria's hand began to itch and the urge to slap Sally grew.

Instead, Gloria cut her off. "I think you're jealous of Andrea," she said bluntly.

Chapter 23

Sally's jaw dropped. "Why I..." she sputtered.

"That's what I thought." Gloria reached down and grabbed a basket from the rack next to her. "I have a few things to pick up and I'm hoping by the time I reach the counter, you'll have something nice to say." Without waiting for a reply, Gloria spun around and marched to the other side of the store.

Gloria fumed as she walked up and down the aisles, blindly grabbing a box of pasta, a jar of spaghetti sauce and a loaf of garlic bread from the freezer. She strode over to the deli counter and thank goodness, Sally wasn't manning the back, as well.

An unfamiliar, smiling face peeked over the top of the counter and two warm gray eyes met hers. "Can I help you?"

Gloria shifted her basket. "Yes. I need six thin slices of Swiss cheese, six slices of smoked gouda and six slices of extra sharp cheddar."

"Coming right up."

Gloria shifted her basket and studied the offerings as she waited for the cheese. The Canadian style bacon looked tempting so she ordered a half a pound, along with a pound of low sodium roasted turkey breast.

The employee, a person Gloria had never seen before, placed the packets on top of the counter. "Anything else?"

"That'll be it." She thanked him and then wandered down the chip aisle, grabbing a bag of wavy potato chips, some tortilla chips and Paul's favorite, spicy jalapeno snack crackers. He loved to eat them with Alice's "special" salsa that Gloria had secretly nicknamed "firecracker."

Sally had calmed down by the time Gloria reached the checkout counter. She pulled the items from the basket and placed them on the counter. "Congratulations on your engagement," she said sincerely, a wave of guilt washing over her at how angry she had gotten over Sally's snide comments.

"Thanks," Sally said. "I know a couple of guys here in town who applied for the job at the hardware store. They said they had lost their jobs at the big box home improvement store over in Rapid Creek."

Gloria fished inside her purse, pulled out her wallet and handed Sally two crisp twenty-dollar bills. "Oh really? Who was it?"

"Mark Clawson for one. He was also working at Fred Baird's sawmill before it closed down. There was another one, but I can't remember his name." Sally punched the buttons on the cash register and the drawer popped open. "There was also Kate Edelson. I was hoping Brian would hire her and get her out of my hair!"

Kate Edelson was Bea McQueen's daughter. Bea was the local hairdresser. Kate worked part-time at the Quik Stop and a few months back, Sally and Kate had gotten into a knockdown, drag out brawl on the grocery store floor.

Gloria thanked her, reached for her bag of groceries and headed out the door. She wondered if Brian had interviewed Mark Clawson. She added both Mark and Kate to her list of suspects, although she doubted it was Kate.

She made her way to the SUV to drop off her purchases and then headed to the post office. There was a long line at the counter and Gloria hovered near the bulletin board, studying the postings until the crowd cleared out.

After the last person exited the building, Gloria approached the counter and leaned her elbows on top. "Sally told me a couple locals applied for the part-time position at the hardware store."

"Uh-huh," Ruth nodded. "Did she tell you her younger brother, Dylan, applied for the job too?"

Gloria lifted a brow. "No, she did not!"

"Yeah. Sally's brother, Dylan, has the hots for Kate and the feeling isn't mutual. Kate is in here every day complaining about how Dylan hangs around the grocery store."

Ruth continued. "Have you talked to Gladys yet?"

Gloria pushed her purse to the side of the counter. "Yeah. I stopped by the drugstore before the Quik Stop." She shook her head. "Whew! She is a woman of few words."

Ruth drummed her fingernails on the countertop. "Gladys grandson, Chad, also applied for the job. I heard from Judith Arnett that Brian immediately dismissed him as a possible hire."

"Why?"

"Because he has a troubled past and was released from prison a few months back. According to one of my sources, who stopped by this morning, Brian ran background checks on all the potential hires and immediately nixed Chad."

Gloria remembered the scar on Gladys' face, how she was a relative unknown in Belhaven and now she had a grandson with a murky past. Still, it didn't mean Gladys had anything to do with the robbery.

There was also Dylan, Sally's younger brother. Why hadn't Sally mentioned her brother had applied? Next was Mark Clawson. Gloria had heard his name before but not in a good – or a bad – way.

"Motive and opportunity," Gloria said. "Motive – robbery. Opportunity – an empty hardware store, with just the owner, early in the morning."

She lifted her index finger. "So we've got the guy who broke out of prison, Walter something, who is on the loose and may have come after Brian. We've got Kate Edelson, although I'm putting her at the bottom of the list."

Ruth interrupted. "Let me grab a sheet of paper." She pulled a small pad from the drawer in front of her and a pen sitting on the counter. "Walter something, Kate Edelson, Glady's grandson, Chad, and Mark Clawson, a local." She paused and looked at Gloria. "Who was the last one?"

"Sally's brother, Dylan," Gloria said. "Five suspects. Could be more. We need to figure out who may have been in the vicinity the morning of the robbery and also if Brian had scheduled interviews that fateful morning." She slammed her fist on the counter. "I wish I could get my hands on the black book – Brian's appointment scheduler – to check it out!"

"We can try the direct approach. March right over to his house and tell him to look for the black book," Ruth said. "Or we can sit back and wait for Brian's memory to return."

"He already told Andrea and all of us in a roundabout way, he wants some space." Gloria said.

Ruth tapped the end of the pen on top of the pad of paper. "I've been giving this some thought. Brian hasn't seen me yet and probably doesn't remember me, either," Ruth replied. "I've never been inside Brian's house. Can you draw a quick sketch of the floor plan?"

***

Ruth turned into Brian Sellers' driveway and parked the U.S. Postal Service vehicle in front of the garage door. It had taken some wheedling on her part to convince Kenny Webber, Belhaven's rural route carrier, to allow her to use his beloved route vehicle. It was his baby and no one drove it but Kenny, until now.

She grabbed the stack of envelopes addressed to Nails and Knobs from the passenger seat and climbed out the driver's side door. "Here goes nothing," Ruth muttered under her breath as she rounded the front of the vehicle and climbed the porch steps.

According to Gloria's crude sketch, Brian's office – and his appointment scheduler – were down a long hall, near the back of the house.

Ruth tossed around the idea of needing to use the restroom, but quickly rejected the idea. Brian was sharp...too sharp to fall for that. She needed something more believable, something that would compel him to hunt down the scheduler, crack it open and take a look.

It had taken Gloria and her some serious brainstorming to come up with a plan – she only hoped it would work. It was all on Ruth now and she was determined to execute the plan flawlessly...now if only Brian would cooperate.

Ruth grasped the stack of envelopes in one hand and pressed the doorbell with the other. *"Da-da-da-dum."* The faint strains of Beethoven's 5th symphony echoed through the door and Ruth smiled.

The door abruptly opened and Ruth took a step backward, almost falling off the porch. She grabbed the handrail to steady herself.

"Can I help you?" Brian peered at Ruth through the screen door.

"Yes. Uh. I'm not sure if you remember me. I'm Ruth Carpenter, head postmaster at the Belhaven Post Office." She waved the stack of mail in her hand. "The mail for the hardware store is piling up. I thought I would bring it by, just in case you wanted to look at it."

Brian unlocked the screen door and held it open. "Thanks." He waved her in.

Ruth stepped into the light and bright, modern living room. It was stunning with its vaulted ceilings and dark wood beams, decorated in a style she loved. This house would be right up her alley. "What a beautiful home. Did you design this yourself?"

Brian shifted his focus and studied the room. "I can't remember. I would like to think I did." He shrugged. "Either way, I like it."

"Oh. Before I forget." Ruth held out the stack of envelopes.

"Thank you." Brian took the mail and gazed at the envelope on top. He rifled through the pile. "These look like job applications."

"That's what I thought," Ruth agreed. "Would you like Kenny, our rural route carrier, to deliver your mail until you return to work?"

"I..." Brian rubbed his brow. "No. I'll start picking it up at the post office, if that's what I used to do."

"You did. You have one PO Box, and use it for the drug store, the Quik Stop and the hardware store."

A flicker of something crossed his face. "I wish I could remember what happened. This is so frustrating." He ran a hand through his hair.

"May I make a suggestion?" Ruth asked.

"Sure."

"Well, rumor has it you have a black appointment scheduler in your home office. You keep all of your appointments and such on your iPad."

"If I had an iPad, it's missing now and probably stolen during the robbery." Brian said. "I found a laptop here at the house. I've tried unlocking it to search for clues but for the life of me, I can't remember the password!"

The pieces were beginning to fall into place. Brian had already tried to figure out what happened, but he couldn't because all of the information was either in his missing iPad or in his laptop, which he had no idea how to get into.

Ruth's pulse quickened. "Brian! If you kept the black scheduler book as a backup, you may have the information right under your nose!"

Chapter 24

Ruth knew exactly where the black scheduler book was – in Brian's home office, but she couldn't tell him that! She glanced at her watch. "I have to get back to work soon, but I have a few extra minutes if you'd like me to help you search for it."

Brian frowned. "You don't have to do that."

Ruth leaned casually against the wall, feigning nonchalance, but she could see her opportunity slipping away. "Sure. But even if you find the book and it lists your schedule for the day of the robbery." She pointed to the stack of envelopes. "If you were interviewing for a position that morning, it's possible you won't have any idea who those people are."

She quickly continued. "I might be able to help since I know almost everyone in town."

Brian rocked back on his heels and rubbed his chin thoughtfully. "You have a point." He shrugged. "I guess it won't hurt to look for the book."

Ruth slowly surveyed the room. "Do you have a home office or computer desk?"

"Yep. Follow me." Brian waved her toward the back of the house. "I have a desk in the corner of the kitchen and also a home office."

They strolled into the kitchen. Ruth stood off to the side while Brian sifted through the desk drawers and then the cupboard above. There was no black book. Ruth knew it wouldn't be there because Andrea had told them Brian kept it in his office.

"What about the office?" she asked.

"It's back here." Brian headed down the long hall and Ruth followed behind him. He opened the door at the end of the hall, ran his hand along the wall and flipped the light switch.

Bright fluorescent light illuminated the masculine room. The centerpiece of the room was a massive mahogany desk. Behind the desk was a large leather office chair. Floor to ceiling bookcases lined one wall. Behind the desk was a bay window that overlooked the lake.

On the other side of the room was a fireplace. On top of the fireplace was a carved mantle, which matched the mahogany desk. Facing the fireplace were two oversized chairs.

"What a beautiful office," Ruth said.

"Thanks. I love it." He shuffled over to the desk and began opening drawers. "Nothing on this side."

He pushed the desk chair back and shifted to the other side. "Aha!" Brian pulled out a large black book and held it up. "I think I found it!"

Ruth eagerly hurried over to the desk and stood off to the side while Brian opened the black book and leaned forward. He flipped a couple pages and then ran his finger down the page. "It happened last Tuesday?"

"Yes." Ruth leaned closer, trying to catch a glimpse of the meticulously handwritten notes. "What does it say?"

"It looks like I had scheduled three interviews that morning." Brian rattled off the names. He told her the times of the appointments and the name of each person.

Ruth began to pace the floor, thinking aloud. "Well, if it was the first person, the second and third person would have shown up after it happened."

"The police told me a customer found me," Brian said.

"It could be the other prospective employees showed up after the customer found you unconscious on the floor and we just don't know it."

"True," Brian agreed. "What if it wasn't one of the prospective employees but someone else?"

Ruth abruptly stopped. There was only one way to find out. "I left my cell phone in the vehicle. Let me make a quick call. I need to get a second opinion." She didn't wait for a reply and darted out of the room, down the hall, through the living room, out the front steps and to the postal vehicle. She opened the passenger side door and pulled her cell phone from the front pocket of her jacket.

Gloria was inside the post office, waiting for Ruth to return when her cell phone began to ring. She pulled it from her purse and stared at the screen. It was Ruth. "Well?"

"Brian found his black book. He had scheduled three job interviews the morning of the robbery. Now what?"

"Let me think!" Gloria stared sightlessly across the street at Dot's Restaurant. "We set up a sting. Flush out the killer." Gloria rattled off some details. "You'll have to somehow convince Brian to go along with the plan."

Ruth squeezed her eyes shut and then opened them. "Somehow, I had a feeling you were going to say that. Okay. I'll see what I can do." She disconnected the line, took a deep breath and headed back inside.

"Brian...I have an idea," Ruth called out as she headed down the long hallway to the office in the back.

***

Gloria was anxious to put the plan into motion, to uncover the culprit, but first, they had to lay the groundwork, and to do that, she needed some backup, namely The Garden Girls, so she called an emergency meeting at Dot's Restaurant.

Gloria briefly explained the plan to each of the girls. The plan was simple and Ruth had been able to convince Brian to play along. Dot and Rose, along with Ruth, would spread a rumor around town that Brian's memory had partially returned and he was returning to work the following morning.

While the girls met to discuss details, Brian contacted the three people who had been scheduled to come in for an interview the morning of the attack. Thankfully, he had meticulously jotted down each person's cell phone number next to his or her name.

Gloria was excited Brian was going to help them attempt to uncover the robbery suspect. Not only that, she hoped his returning to the hardware store might somehow "jog" his memory.

The plan was for Brian to confront each of the suspects, pretending to remember what had happened and naming each of them as his attacker.

Gloria hoped the bluff would work and one of them would confess. Meanwhile she, along with Lucy, who would be packing heat, would be close by and ready for the takedown once the culprit confessed.

Gloria didn't have a "Plan B" if none of them confessed.

"Do you think you should ask Officer Joe Nelson to be your back-up?" Dot, the ever-sensible one, asked.

It wasn't a bad idea, and the more Gloria thought about it, the more she decided they should ask him.

"What if he takes over our sting operation?" Lucy argued. "I won't get to use my gun or anything."

"Are you crazy?" Margaret gasped. "What if you lure the perp back to the scene of the crime and he decides to finish the job and shoot Brian?"

Lucy shook her head. "Not if I shoot him…or her – first."

The girls argued back and forth, about the merits of including Officer Nelson in the sting operation. Gloria could see both sides and she was firmly on the fence. "Why don't we let Brian decide? After all, it's his safety and his business."

"I'll call him." Since Ruth was Brian's point of contact and the one who had convinced him to give their scheme a shot, they let her make the call. "I have to get back to work right now but I'll let you know what he says as soon as I talk to him." She scrambled out of the chair, grabbed her purse and hurried to the door.

Gloria watched her leave and then pushed her own chair back. "In the meantime, I'm going to give Andrea a call to make sure she made it safely to Nantucket."

Lucy followed Gloria's lead. "I'm going to go home and do some practice shooting. It's a shame Andrea isn't here. She could shoot with me." Andrea loved to shoot guns, and Lucy and she spent a couple afternoons a month at Lucy's makeshift shooting range out behind her house.

The girls parted ways with Dot and Rose promising to spread the good news about Brian's recovery. Margaret left at the same time as Lucy and Gloria, and she followed them out the front door. "Is there anything I can do to help?" she asked.

Gloria frowned. Margaret was usually one of the last to be asked and not because she wasn't willing to pitch in on investigations, covert operations and stakeouts, it was just that the others had honed a skill that typically came in handy.

Lucy was the weapons expertise, Dot with her restaurant where she could glean information and spread rumors, when necessary. Ruth, of course, had an ideal position where she had insider information on everything that happened in their small town, not to mention her surveillance background and her arsenal of spy equipment.

She remembered their last investigation, how Margaret had been so excited to try to hypnotize Eleanor Whittaker to help her remember. Gloria knew Margaret was anxious to be included in the sting but wasn't sure how she could help.

Gloria gazed down the sidewalk, toward the hardware store. "If you want, you can be our lookout, someone nearby who can keep an eye on whoever enters the store."

"Record them?" Margaret asked eagerly. "I just got one of those fancy new smartphones and this baby is a real gem. I can record the whole thing," she gushed.

It certainly wouldn't hurt to have another set of boots on the ground so-to-speak, and Gloria wanted Margaret to feel included.

"Perfect," Gloria said. "We'll have you close by, maybe across the street from the hardware store. "Let's go scope it out."

Lucy headed to her jeep while Gloria and Margaret hustled down the sidewalk to the hardware store at the end of the block. They crossed the street and made their way over to the old, abandoned Masonic Temple.

The temple...what was left of it...was a disaster. It had mysteriously burned a few years back. Rumor had it someone had set the place on fire, but the initial investigation had quickly fallen to the wayside and finally fizzled. In Gloria's opinion, it was an eyesore and a safety hazard for the children in the area.

She wished they would raze the building. The freemasons and temple itself were always somewhat of a mystery. Some of the locals attended but it was a "members only" organization. Gloria left well enough alone and never gave it much thought.

Gloria studied what was left of the windows, and could see daylight on the other side. She lowered her gaze and studied the building's foundation. "This would be the best spot to hang out but it is a little creepy."

Margaret shrugged. "Doesn't bother me at all. I can hide my SUV in the parking lot on the other side."

The women tiptoed around the ruins and stopped on the other side near what was once the main entrance. One entire section of the wall had collapsed.

"I don't know Margaret. This doesn't look safe." Gloria shivered. "Not only that, it's giving me the willies."

Margaret stuck her foot out and poked around the rubble, surveying the charred ruins. "I found a spot I can hide out. Don't worry about me."

The women retraced their steps and stopped in front of Dot's Restaurant and the SUV. "What time should I be in place?" Margaret asked.

"We're going to meet Brian at the hardware store at 7:30 in the morning, half an hour before he's scheduled to open."

"Sounds good." Margaret nodded. "I'll plan on being in position by 7:45." She patted her purse. "We haven't had this much excitement since…"

"Since Ed Mueller's body was found in the ice shanty out on the lake earlier this year," Gloria said.

"You're right! It seems so long ago."

Margaret hopped into her SUV, gave Gloria a small salute and then drove off.

Gloria watched until her vehicle disappeared over the top of the hill. "I'm getting a bad feeling about this one," she groaned as she slid behind the wheel and reached for her seatbelt.

Chapter 25

The first thing Gloria did when she arrived at the farm was to let Mally out for a run. She settled into the rocker on the porch and dialed Andrea's cell phone.

A breathless Andrea picked up on the second ring. "Hello?"

"Hello dear. It's me. Gloria. I wanted to call to make sure you landed safely."

"Oh yes! I'm here. I had forgotten how beautiful Nantucket was in the late spring. You should see it."

Gloria had never been to Nantucket. In fact, she'd never been to the State of Massachusetts. It sounded lovely. Gloria had a long bucket list of places she wanted to visit before she died. Paul and she had tossed around the idea of spending the fall driving up the east coast during color touring season.

He had suggested renting an RV for a couple months. After honeymooning in an RV, Gloria knew she would enjoy it as much, if not more, than staying in a hotel. It would be a kind of home away from home. They had set a tentative date, the months of September and October, but that was as far as they had gotten with the plans.

"I'm glad you're enjoying yourself Andrea." She wasn't sure whether she should mention Brian and decided to let her friend bring up his name, which after several minutes of chitchat, she did.

"How is Brian?"

"He's hanging around his home. Ruth stopped by there this morning to drop off his mail." She went on to tell Andrea how Ruth had convinced him to track down the black book, his scheduler. "We were right. Brian had scheduled three interviews the morning of his attack." Gloria told Andrea they had set up a sting for the following morning and Brian was all in.

"He wouldn't let me try to help but was more than willing to let all of you," Andrea said sadly.

"Remember, Andrea, Brian didn't remember Ruth. To him, she was an outsider and not someone he supposedly already knew."

"True." Andrea let out a sigh. "Good luck. Keep me posted."

After they said their good-byes, Gloria wasn't sure if it had been a good idea to share their plan and Brian's involvement since it seemed to have only made Andrea feel even more isolated from the man she loved.

Gloria offered a quick prayer for Brian's speedy recovery and then headed inside to fix lunch.

***

"You said Margaret is across the street hanging out in the creepy old burned out building keeping an eye on this place?" Lucy asked in a loud whisper.

Gloria placed her eye against the keyhole and peered out. She could just make out Brian as he moved back and forth behind the counter.

"Yeah. I drove by on my way here. Her vehicle is parked out back, behind a tree."

Gloria turned her attention to her friend. "You bring your gun?"

"Yep." Lucy patted her purse. "Maybe I should get it out, get ready in case I need to shoot someone."

"Please don't shoot yourself...or me," Gloria glanced nervously at Lucy's purse.

Gloria kept a gun in her nightstand next to her bed. It wasn't loaded. She was afraid one of her grandsons would come over and find the loaded firearm and she would never forgive herself if that happened.

Paul had promised to teach the boys how to shoot, with their parent's permission, of course. Tyler was at an age where he would be able to handle the instructions. Ryan, in her opinion, was still a little too young.

When Paul had mentioned taking Tyler deer hunting in the fall, her grandson hadn't forgotten it and every time he saw Paul, he reminded him.

Gloria turned her attention to the keyhole. "Oh! Someone just walked in." Her armpits grew damp and her heart pounded in her chest as a pair of khaki slacks came into view.

"Let me see."

She shifted to the side and Lucy peered through the hole. "We should've borrowed some of Ruth's spy equipment."

"It's a little too late now," Gloria whispered. The girls grew silent as they listened to the exchange on the other side of the door.

Brian had rattled off the schedule when the girls first arrived. Dylan Wells, Sally's younger brother, would be the first to arrive. Brian and Dylan chatted for what seemed like forever.

Sharp pains began to shoot up Gloria's legs as she crouched on her knees.

"I can't take this." She groaned and then plopped over onto her butt.

Lucy gazed at her friend. "What if he starts attacking Brian and I need to come to his aid?"

"I'll roll out of the way," Gloria promised.

Loud voices on the other side of the door caught their attention. "You're crazy dude! That knock on your noggin messed you up!" The young man, Dylan, stormed down the center aisle, flung the front door open and slammed it shut behind him.

"That ended badly," Lucy reported. She glanced at her watch: 8:25. "When is the next person supposed to show up?"

"Kate Edelson is scheduled to stop by at eight thirty and the last person, Mark Clawson, is coming in at nine o'clock." Her greatest fear was nothing would happen and they would be back to square one with no suspects and Brian's memory as fuzzy as a ripe peach on a hot Georgia summer day.

At approximately eight twenty-nine, Kate entered through the front door. She strolled to the back, hopped up on a barstool and watched Brian as he waited on a customer who had wandered in.

"What's happening?" Gloria asked anxiously.

"Brian is waiting on a customer. Kate is sitting on a barstool," Lucy reported.

The customer finally exited the building, and Kate and Brian were all alone.

Gloria and Lucy switched places as Gloria peeked through the key hole. "What is she doing?" she muttered under her breath.

Kate hopped off the barstool, rounded the side of the bar and disappeared from sight.

Gloria grasped the doorknob, gently twisted and eased the door open, praying it wouldn't creak.

She could see Kate now, clear as a bell. She was standing mere inches from Brian, leaning forward while Brian was leaning back in an attempt to put some distance between them.

Kate was hitting on Brian! It was like a chess game. She moved forward. He shuffled back and almost lost his balance as he reached for the counter behind him.

"I know you remember, Brian. Give me three seconds to prove it to you," Kate purred as she grabbed Brian's arm and pulled him toward her. She tilted her head and puckered up for a kiss that didn't happen.

"I don't..."

Kate's expression changed in a flash. "Don't what? I think you do remember and this amnesia bull crap is your way of pretending you didn't have the hots for me," she screeched.

"Kate." Brian held up his hands.

Kate pulled her hand back and slapped Brian across the face before stomping out of the hardware store. She slammed the door behind her.

Gloria's eyes widened and she turned to Lucy. "Oh my gosh!" They were sitting on the floor, dumbfounded, when Brian strode over. He looked down at the women sitting cross-legged on the floor.

"The woman, Kate, is off her rocker. I did not have a relationship with her. At least not that I remember. I think I would remember and on top of that, I don't date psychos." Brian began to pace the floor.

Gloria was about to reply when her cell phone vibrated. It was Margaret. "Hello?"

"Gloria! You've gotta get out of there!"

Chapter 26

Margaret yelled into the phone. At that precise moment, the back storeroom window shattered, spraying shards of glass across the floor. *"Ping! Ping!"*

"Someone is shooting at us!" Brian yelled.

Things moved fast after that. Lucy scampered across the floor and out of the room. Brian grabbed Gloria under both arms and dragged her from the room.

He pulled her into the front of the store before pulling the door shut behind them.

"What's going on?" A tall, dark-haired man raced down the center aisle to the back of the store.

"Someone was shooting at us through the back window," Gloria gasped as she rolled over and pushed herself to her feet.

Lucy, who had darted out first, fumbled inside her purse and pulled out her handgun. She tiptoed to the back door and grasped the door handle, keeping a tight grip on her weapon.

"Be careful Lucy." Brian started to follow behind and then abruptly stopped. "Hey! I remember. I remember you!"

"Do you remember me?" Gloria asked.

"Not...yet Ginger," he admitted.

The young man ducked down and hid behind the counter. Gloria wondered if he was Mark Clawson, the last applicant. Her eyes narrowed and she watched as he peeked over the edge of the counter. Had he shot at them through the window and then decided to run inside and become some sort of "hero?"

He looked innocent enough.

Gloria's phone beeped. It was Margaret. "Are you guys okay?"

"Yes," Gloria let out the breath she'd been holding. "What about you?"

"I'm fine," Margaret said. "The person who shot at the hardware store, they took off."

Gloria turned to Lucy. "Let's step outside while they chat." The women exited through the front door and Gloria began to pace up and down the sidewalk. Perhaps it had been Kate Adelson. She seemed ticked off Brian had rebuffed her advances.

A figure darted out from behind the burned out Masonic Temple and ran across the street. It was Margaret. "Someone shot out the side window."

"Yeah. There are shards of glass everywhere but no one got hit," Lucy said.

Gloria stopped pacing and turned to Margaret. "Did you see who fired the shots?"

"I'm sorry Gloria. I was looking down at my phone. The battery was getting low and I was trying to figure out how much time I had left. When I looked up, I caught a glimpse of a vehicle stopped in the road next to the hardware store." Margaret laced her fingers together. "I didn't see a person, but I did see the back of a red sports car as it sped away."

Gloria began to pace again. "There's something, some small clue nagging at the back of my mind."

The dark-haired man, who had raced inside right after the gunman shot out the store windows, emerged from the hardware store. He stopped to talk to the girls. "I think I'm cursed." He glanced back at the hardware store door.

"I wouldn't blame Mr. Sellers for not hiring me. From the look on his face, he thinks I was the one who shot out the window. I get the feeling he thinks I'm some sort of stalker madman." While the young man talked, his words were like a lightning bolt that ignited Gloria's mind.

She reached out to touch his arm. "That's it! I know who's behind all this and I'm convinced beyond a shadow of a doubt it's not you!"

Gloria raced up the steps and burst through the front door of the hardware store. "I know who attacked you and who shot at the back of the store!"

Her words tumbled out as she continued. "The car that Margaret spotted. I would bet a million bucks it's parked down at the grocery store," she said.

Lucy hovered in the doorway listening.

Gloria spun around. "Tell Mark that Brian will be in touch and then lock the front door."

"Let's go!" Brian grabbed his keys and headed to the back. Lucy locked the front door and the women hurried down the center aisle. Brian, Lucy and Gloria, along with Margaret, who met them out back, hopped into his pick-up truck.

"Circle around the block so we can see the back of the Quik Stop," Gloria said.

Brian stomped on the gas, raced to the stop sign, careened around the corner and hit the gas again. They reached the back of the corner grocery seconds later.

There, parked next to Sally Keane's beat-up four-door sedan, was a bright red sports car.

"It was Dylan Wells, Sally Keane's brother?" Lucy guessed.

"I'm calling the cops," Brian pulled his cell phone from his front pocket and dialed 911. "Yes. This is Brian Sellers. We have an armed robbery suspect and gunman cornered. We need police right away." He rattled off the address before reaching for the driver's side door handle.

"I'm going to punch his lights out!"

"I don't think..." Gloria's voice trailed off.

Brian shoved the driver's side door open. In his haste, he didn't notice the utility pole next to the driver's side door. The door whacked the pole with brute force, swung back and hit Brian in the side of the head.

"Uh!" Brian grabbed his head, tumbled out of the truck and crumpled to the ground.

Gloria vaulted over the center console and into the driver's seat. She stuck her head out the door. Brian was lying on the edge of the road, his eyes closed.

"Oh my gosh! Brian! Brian!" Gloria scrambled out of the vehicle, dropped to her knees and grabbed Brian's hand. "Brian. Can you hear me?"

By now, Lucy and Margaret had jumped out of the back of the vehicle and hovered over his still body.

Gloria touched his cheek and leaned close to Brian's face. "Brian, can you hear me?"

Brian let out a low moan. His eyes fluttered and then opened. He reached up and touched his forehead. "Gloria? What happened?"

Chapter 27

The police showed up in a caravan of cop cars, lights flashing, and arrested Dylan Wells for armed robbery and attempted murder. After the arrest, Gloria drove Brian, who complained of a bad headache, back to his house.

She waited until Alice, who had not gone in to work, arrived to keep an eye on him.

Gloria wondered if perhaps the second bump to Brian's head caused his amnesia to disappear. Alice, thrilled that Brian's memory had returned, swore up and down her special soup had finally worked its magic.

The girls gathered at Dot's Restaurant shortly after the arrest and Brian was safely at home resting. "How did you know it was Sally's brother?" Dot poured each of the girls a cup of coffee and set the empty pot in the center of the table.

"Well, I knew there was some clue, hovering in the back of my mind, something Mark Clawson said that caused the light bulb to go on. He said something to the effect Brian must have thought he was cursed or some sort of stalker."

Gloria sipped her coffee and gazed at Ruth over the rim. "Then I remembered how Ruth had said that Dylan was obsessed with Kate Edelson, who worked with his sister, Sally, at the grocery store. Kate was all over Brian in the hardware store. My theory is somehow, Dylan found out Kate was infatuated with Brian, so he decided to attack Brian and make it look like a robbery."

"But money was missing from the cash register," Margaret pointed out.

"Yes, but not Brian's wallet." Gloria pointed out. "Why would someone rob Brian and not take his wallet, including any cash, credit cards, etc.? It didn't add up."

"Ah." Rose crossed her arms and leaned back in the chair. "Brian's memory is back, thanks to my special memory potion."

"Or the second bump on the noggin," Lucy said.

"Or Alice's spicy soup," Ruth added.

"Or all of the above," Dot finished.

"What about Andrea? Shouldn't we call her?" Lucy asked.

Gloria grinned. "Brian asked if he could make the call."

"Aww." The girls became misty-eyed at the thought of Brian calling his beloved to let her know his memory had returned and to find out when she was coming home.

"Well, I better get going." Gloria eased out of the chair, grabbed her purse and limped around the side of the table.

"What's wrong?" Dot asked. "Why are you limping?"

"I'm getting old," Gloria joked. "Rolling around on the hardware store floor and then running back and forth didn't help, either."

Rose hopped out of her chair, pushing it back. "Well, Gloria, this is your lucky day. I have just the cure for that!" She held up an index finger. "Don't go anywhere. I'll be right back!"

The end.

The Series Continues...Book 14 Coming Soon!

If you enjoyed reading "Forget Me Knot" please take a moment to leave a review. It would be greatly appreciated! Thank you!

Chicken Tortilla Casserole Recipe

Ingredients:
2 Tablespoons chicken broth or water
8 ounce carton of sour cream or plain yogurt
10 ¾ ounce can cream of mushroom soup
16 ounce jar mild, medium or hot chunky salsa*
12 flour tortillas cut into strips
4 cups diced and cooked chicken or turkey
4 cups shredded cheddar cheese

Directions:
-Preheat oven to 350 degrees.
-Grease 9"x13" baking dish.
-Spoon water or broth into dish.
-In bowl, mix sour cream, mushroom soup and salsa.
-Layer 1/3 of the tortilla strips, 1/3 of chicken, 1/3 of soup mixture and 1/3 of cheese. Repeat two times.
-Bake at 350 degrees for 40 minutes.
-Let stand 10 – 15 minutes before serving.

*To add some extra heat, substitute ¼ of the salsa with Texas Pete.